Powder River

Center Point
Large Print

Also by Francis W. Hilton and available from Center Point Large Print:

The Mañana Kid
Phantom Rustlers

This Large Print Book carries the Seal of Approval of N.A.V.H.

Powder River

Francis W. Hilton

Center Point Large Print
Thorndike, Maine

This Center Point Large Print edition
is published in the year 2024 by arrangement with
Golden West Inc.

Originally published in the US by H. C. Kinsey &
Company, Inc.

The text of this Large Print edition is unabridged.
In other aspects, this book may vary
from the original edition.
Printed in the United States of America
on permanent paper sourced using
environmentally responsible foresting methods.
Set in 16-point Times New Roman type.

ISBN 979-8-89164-072-6 (hardcover)
ISBN 979-8-89164-076-4 (paperback)

The Library of Congress has cataloged this record
under Library of Congress Control Number: 2023950457

Powder River

CHAPTER I

In silence two men rode through the May twilight, hoof-beats drumming hollowly on the chalk bluffs. Where the dusty trail pitched down through a gap in the gyp cap-rock to the Belle Fourche River, their mounts snorted and lunged back. Sharp rowels urged them ahead. On their rumps they gained a bench above the sluggish stream. Here the elder of the riders jerked a thumb to the right. Without a word his companion yanked rope on a lagging pack-horse and followed along a trail that twisted beside the river.

Presently the old man drew rein and pointed ahead. Far up the valley a scatter of lights, pale and wan as the first stars slipping into the evening sky, twinkled through the purple haze.

"Yonder is the town of Halfway, stranger," he said. "But if I were you and didn't have good reason for going in I'd shag right along this bench and pass it up."

"Why?"

The abrupt query by his companion, a broad-shouldered, lean-hipped young cowboy, might have been only to encourage conversation. For it was carelessly indifferent—as had been every word he had uttered since riding into a line camp deep in the Belle Fourche brakes that afternoon.

He had only asked direction to Halfway, sought no other information, volunteered none. The rangey, slash-faced sorrel gelding he rode, with the easy grace of one born to the saddle, carried six brands, all foreign. Dry lather webbed the brute's flanks and matted the mane behind its ears; his pack-horse moved on leaden legs. Dust on the rider's heat-curled chaps, gray flannel shirt and hat were further evidence of a long, hard trail. But he had given no sign of weariness. His grim lips divulged nothing. The determined set to his square jaws invited no question even in the lonely line shack, where the old man was breaking camp.

As they drew rein now on the banks of the river the youth crooked a cramped leg about the saddle-horn, eased his other foot from a sweaty stirrup and lifted his hat to brush sunburned sandy hair back from a high, sweat-beaded brow.

His companion, a stocky white-haired man of wrinkled, wind-pitted countenance, who carried the weight of years surprisingly well, leaned over in the saddle, plucked a stalk of bunch grass and chewed on it the while his inquisitive gaze swept the deeply-tanned face of the cowboy. A boyishly-pleasant, clear-cut face it was, which had but shed the down of youth, yet withal was hard-lined. . . . The face of a youth who had lived and seen much, strong, capable of masking any emotion.

"There are a good many reasons for passing up Halfway," the old fellow shrugged presently. "That might be one of them."

Gray eyes followed the direction he indicated; cool, gray eyes, fearless, steady, in the depths of which lurked a pin-point of light that could, one sensed, flare into a savage glitter. Tacked to a fence post ahead was a weather-beaten placard. The youth dropped the lead rope of the pack-horse. Booted feet found stirrups. Long-shanked spurs, with dime-thin rowels, brought a snort from his mount as they lifted the brute forward.

$1,000 REWARD

ONE THOUSAND DOLLARS WILL BE PAID FOR INFORMATION LEADING TO THE ARREST AND CONVICTION OF THE MURDERER OF JACK HALLIDAY, FOREMAN OF THE ROCKING CHAIR RANCH, ON DEC . . .

Storm and sun had obliterated the rest. The youth shot an inscrutable glance at his companion. Then he shifted sidewise in his saddle, weight in one stirrup, to whip his gaze over the region.

Across the river rose the heavily-timbered Black Hills, great somber piles in the twilight haze. Opposite towered the Bear Lodge mountains, gigantic purple shafts, sharp-etched against the orange sky. Ahead and behind rolled the Belle Fourche basin, walled in by multi-colored bluffs, boulder-littered gashed by sluggish water. Flat-topped buttes reared up from the level floor, oddly shaped, gray, ugly.

The old man spat out the grass savagely and rummaged in the overalls beneath his ancient barrel-legged chaps to drag forth a cob pipe and dirty plug.

"I'm not saying that is all the reason for staying away from Halfway, you understand," he offered guardedly. "Folks who live in these parts don't do any more talking than they have to." He pared a slice from the plug, rubbed the tobacco into a crumbly ball between horny palms, stuffed it tight into the bowl, brushed off his hands and lighted it. "But Halfway isn't just what you'd call a healthy hangout for strangers. Specially right now."

"Why?" Again the abrupt query was the only evidence the young cowboy was even listening.

The old man sucked furiously until his pipe was sending up a fog of rank smoke. "There's hell popping in this country of late. Take the Rocking Chair ranch, old Chris Nathan's spread just across the line in the Dakota Bear Lodge for instance. Been having a heap of trouble . . . Killed Jack Halliday, the foreman . . ." He jerked a thumb toward the weather-beaten placard.

"On top of that Chris lost a thousand head of prime critters going to summer range on Powder River last spring. Chris always summers on Big Powder. . . . That's just a couple of the things, but it seems like . . ." He checked himself abruptly as though he already had revealed too much. "There's a carnival in there at Halfway now. . . . The toughest hands in the country are there. . . . The lid's off. . . . The sky's the limit."

If his companion caught the veiled warning, it was obvious his words were intended to convey, he gave no sign. For his gaze remained fixed on the purple Bear Lodge, now swiftly melting away into the darkened sky.

"There was a time when there was peace and order in these parts." From beneath shaggy brows the old rancher studied the untalkative cowboy who sat his mount, straight as a sapling, the thumb of his right hand hooked in a studded cartridge belt with tied-down holster and jutting forty-five Colt. "That was when Jack Halliday was alive. That reward shows how popular Jack was—the finest fellow who ever lived—but plumb poison to hoot-owlers. They came to hate him, because he stood for law and order. They finally got him. . . . Like they get all good men in this country—Murdered him in cold blood. . . . Damn their souls, I . . ." Again he caught himself. "It isn't any of my affair, you understand, stranger, but I was mighty close to old Jack

Halliday. I see things that probably nobody else in this country would see. . . ."

"That being?" There was a note of challenge in the cowboy's soft-spoken interruption.

"That being just a trace of resemblance between you and old Jack Halliday. There's always been gossip that Jack had a son. It wouldn't be very healthy for any kin of Jack Halliday's in Halfway—specially playing a lone hand."

The cowboy jerked his gray eyes from the mountains to meet the old fellow's inquisitive gaze. "I was raised in Montana. How far is it to Halfway?"

"Five miles straight up this trail. But it's a hard one, I'm telling you, stranger. And I'm saying if a square-eyed, clean-cut young jasper like you has got business in other parts, you had better tend to it first—Halfway is the hell-hole of the Bear Lodge."

"Much obliged." The cowboy recovered the lead rope of his pack-horse, which had wandered off to graze, and tightened rein. "Mebbeso I'll drift back this way some time. If I do, I'll look you up. So-long!"

"So-long!" The old man extended his hand, pulled his pony about.

The youth watched him until he had disappeared around a jagged chalk bluff. Then he roweled on along the trail that led up the valley.

Closer now and more brightly in the creeping

shadows twinkled the lights of Halfway. On the evening breeze came faintly the sounds of shouts, the occasional report of a gun, muffled with distance.

A ragged, meandering trail gashed with innumerable flood washes; a trail of endless pitches and stiff climbs, and then his sorrel was sidling nervously up the dusty street of the village, lighted by the feeble rays of coal oil lamps—glowing from open doorways and filtering through dirty window panes—and by flickering gasoline flares on gaudily decorated booths set in the middle of the narrow street. Gleaming-eyed broncs, lining the hitch-rails, shied and snorted as he rode past. Out of the gloom beyond came the angry squeals of other broncs, fighting savagely.

Locating a livery barn at the head of the street, he roweled his frightened mount and close-snubbed pack-horse beneath the lantern that hung at the entrance, swung down, gave brief instructions for their care and strode stiffly back into the street.

Punchers jostled him on the narrow rickety boardwalk; rough, unshaven punchers, evil-faced, shifty-eyed. Painted, husky-voiced women spoke to him. From the open doorways of restaurants and saloons came the banging of pianos, the scrape of fiddles and booted feet. Hawkers yelled from the bunting-rimmed booths in the middle of the street. About him yowling choruses arose;

maudlin bass and coyote falsetto in ear-splitting discord. The dusk was eerie with yells and whoops. Even the cool breeze that now whipped down from the Bear Lodge to sift the sand, scuffed up by restless feet, against the false fronts of the straggling two score of weather-beaten buildings, lent a mournful wail to the uproar.

Keenly alive to the color, the light about him, thrilled by the noise, he moved along, content to revel in the sight of people—after the manner of men of the silent rangeland who live for the days they can know human companionship. Much as they attracted him he passed up the carnival booths. He elbowed through the crowd of watching town-folk, congregated about the dingy two-story brick courthouse, the barred windows of which showed that it also served as a jail.

Where the street ended abruptly and a yellow ribbon of a trail replaced the rattling plank walk, he crossed over. A church—its spire, sadly in need of shingles, rising into the night—stood before him. Past homes he wandered, dimly-lighted homes where families were gathered about tables. A printer jerking back on the lever of a press held his attention for a moment. Next door a cobbler drew nails from his mouth, setting them with a single rhythmic stroke into the sole of a shoe upturned on the last between his knees. Beyond a burly butcher in a spotted apron alternated between saw and cleaver. . . .

Again he was back in the crowd. With lagging steps he passed up the "Flying Dutchman" saloon, overflowing with cowboys, wild and untamed as the broncs snorting and pawing at the hitch-rails about him. At the end of the street he stopped before the "Double Eagle." Here too was a bedlam of shouts, curses and ribald song. He pushed through the swinging doors into a tight-packed mass and halted.

Howling punchers reeled about him, rowels raking the rough board floor. Punchers hunched over poker tables. Punchers slumped against the long pine bar with knees of tallow. The air reeked with the odor of sweaty leather and stale beer. Halfway, the hell-hole of the Bear Lodge, in carnival spirit, was living up to its reputation.

Crowding through to a lunch counter in the rear, he straddled a stool, gave his order to a shuffling, stoop-shouldered cook in soiled apron, then swung round to watch the yowling mob.

Presently from all the boisterous, milling crowd his eyes singled out one puncher, a giant of a black-muzzled man in bangle-studded chaps and gaudy shirt, slouching against the end of the bar. His face was leathery, corrugated, deep-pitted by wind and sun. Liquor had dulled the glitter of beady black eyes that roved and whipped about restlessly. An ugly smile was set on his thick, weather-cracked lips.

Fascinated by the brutality of that face, the

flashiness of his garb, the newcomer watched him until he hunched about to dash off a stiff drink.

Then his eyes roved on to the back bar, littered with reward notices, pictures of women in tights and prize-fighters in characteristic poses. Many were dingy with age, their names all but obliterated by constant thumbing. But here and there a new beauty, torn from the pages of a pink magazine, showed that the pouchy-faced bartender had an eye for pretty women and still took pride in his gallery of art.

The arrival of his food cut short his survey. Swinging around he fell to it hungrily.

"It's on me!" After a time the big cowboy at the end of the bar shook himself, yanked the ornate-banded hat from his head and let forth a wild yell. "When Ed Jackson and his Rocking Chair gang are in town, everybody drinks." He lurched into the crowd, slapping cowboys on the back, giving them a shove to send them on their weaving way to the bar.

Having finished his meal, the newcomer moved away from the lunch counter to find a chair near the front of the saloon, tilt it against the wall and roll himself a cigaret. There he sat watching curiously.

"Every jasper in the house is invited," the big puncher yowled. "You're all my friends. . . . But ary jasper in Halfway who don't belly up when

Ed Jackson treats I'll . . ." He broke off at sight of the newcomer, the one man in the saloon who made no move to accept the invitation.

"Rear up on your hind legs, stranger!" the puncher, Jackson, ordered angrily. "Ary jasper who don't drink with me—"

The young cowboy made no move. Jackson's coldly glittering eyes swept him from head to foot. He saw a puncher almost as large as himself, broad-shouldered, lean-hipped, lithe-limbed, his deep-tanned features set in an expression almost of amusement. There was about him youth; confident, healthy youth, that somehow seemed strangely out of place. But it was his eyes that captured and held Jackson's baleful glare. They were cool and gray, unflinching, steady. Under different circumstances the almost imperceptible gleam in those eyes might have carried a sinister warning. But liquor had dulled Jackson's sight.

"I said the drinks were on me," he rasped out.

Another clock-tick of deathly silence. The shouts ceased. The crowd whirled to regard the strange youth with astonished awe.

"Thanks just the same," he said lazily. "But I just ate. Besides, I never touch a drop."

"Here's once you do." A malevolent grin twisted Jackson's thick lips. "The jasper who don't drink with Ed Jackson is against him."

"Put it anyway you want to," he answered carelessly.

In half a dozen swift strides, Jackson was above him. One great hairy fist clenched, drew back threateningly.

Not until then did the young cowboy move, with the speed and grace of a puma. Even before his tilted chair banged to the floor he was on his feet. To the astonishment of the crowd he sent his fist crashing to Jackson's unguarded jaw. The fellow rocked on his heels, went lurching backwards to crash against the bar.

"You fouled me, you damned drifter," he choked. "I wasn't ready. . . . I . . ." He started for his gun. But the newcomer had followed up his advantage. A stunning left hook to the mouth stopped him, sent him back against the bar, spitting blood. He shook his head, let forth the bellow of an enraged bull. His right crashed low to double the cowboy up.

The crowd waited for the stranger to go down. That for all the courage he had displayed there was a chance of him whipping the burly, hard-fisted Jackson, terror of the Bear Lodge, was beyond their comprehension. Jackson would stoop to anything. The punch he had just landed was foul. But there was no referee. No man in Halfway dared intercede where Ed Jackson was concerned.

But to the amazement of everyone, the cowboy did not go down. He jerked straight, crossed, shot in a sizzling left. It caught Jackson squarely over the heart. The blow was audible to every corner of the now quiet saloon. It left Jackson gasping. But he stood up under it; leaped out to stand toe to toe, exchanging blows. . . . Swift, terrible punches that would have felled men of lesser brawn.

Then, of a sudden, the stranger picked an uppercut from the floor, plastered it against Jackson's chin. Pent-up breath soughed forth in the nerve-taut crowd. Some even had the temerity to shift a cramped foot.

Jackson swayed on his feet. A left, a right rocked his head from side to side. His eyes were glazed, his expression fixed. He was out on his feet. The stupefied on-lookers now waited for him to go down. The strange cowboy's furious blows gave them confidence. He was spitting blood. One gray eye was closed. But he was smiling broadly.

Clawing blindly for his gun, the punch-drunk Jackson lurched away from the hail of fists. The cowboy followed up, started another blow to his weaving chin. It never landed. Ed Jackson crumpled to the floor of the saloon.

Pandemonium broke loose. From out of the dense-packed crowds came a dolorous and mocking; "One!"

Jackson was on all fours, spewing blood, trying to rise.

"Two!"

The strange cowboy stood over him, ready to send him back down. But Jackson did not rise. With a groan he straightened out and rolled onto his back.

A thunderous cheer shook the rafters of the resort. But the young cowboy ignored the deafening praise. With a shrug he turned away, sauntered to the swinging doors, kicked them open with his knee and went outside, the dumfounded crowd staring after him.

CHAPTER II

Outside the saloon the cowboy paused. Quick eyes, that still glinted dangerously, whipped up and down the dimly-lighted street. But apparently a fight was so common in Halfway it caused no more than a ripple of excitement among those who chanced to witness it.

Straightening his cartridge belt and settling the thonged-down forty-five more comfortably at his hip, he hoisted his chaps with his wrists and strode over to hunch against the corner of the building. Steady fingers found tobacco and papers in the pocket of his shirt. He twisted a cigaret.

The night air was a bedlam of shouts and laughter. The raucous cries of hawkers lured the unwary. Boisterous, yelling crowds still clustered about the booths, their shadows great disproportionate ogres in the flickering light of the breeze-whipped flares. Yet his ear was quick to note the snatches of song were more uncertain, more discordant. Above the delighted shrieks of the merry-makers rose an occasional thick voice in angry challenge as some disgruntled puncher reeled out from the hooting mob.

Keenly conscious of the life and gaiety about him, yet utterly fatigued from long miles in the saddle, the cowboy lighted his cigaret and snapped away the match. He watched it trace a pencil of light into the gloom, glow for an instant in the dust beyond the dilapidated boardwalk. Then turning, he moved down the street, dime-thin rowels tinkling, his gait a shamble in high-heeled boots, yet, withal, noticeably springy and sure.

Reaching the end of the street he located what appeared to be the town's one hotel—the Halfway House—a rambling, ramshackle building of two stories, even more gaunt and weather-beaten than the rest. Casting aside his half-smoked quirly he quickened his pace. It meant rest under a roof.

"What's your hurry, stranger?"

A voice at his elbow brought him whirling about. Quick as a flash his hand fluttered down to rest, one thumb hooked in his cartridge belt. But the man who had accosted him was coolly dragging the "makin's" from a shirt pocket and offering them.

"Don't mind if I do."

The cowboy took the proffered peace sign, the while his gaze jerked over the puncher, a gaunt, gangling man with a long and peaked face. Almost owlish in its solemnity was that face, the color of wet leather, with big round eyes set deep in a mass of gloomy wrinkles. Storm and wind had left the brim of his hat limp as a flopping rag. His garb was dusty, a faded blue shirt thrown open at the throat to reveal a neck blackened and burned, brush-scarred chaps minus all of the bangles that once had made them flashy. Frayed braid on a buttonless vest hinted of better times and a garment's faded glory.

"Stranger in these parts?" The fellow's query in a peculiarly nasal tone, was unmistakably friendly.

"Yeah." The cowboy's hand slid away from his cartridge belt. He backed against a building out of the way of the jostling crowd, tapped out the makin's, twisted a cigaret deftly with one hand, pulled the sack shut with his teeth and passed it back. "Montana."

"Had a hunch from them long shanks and little rowels," the lanky puncher remarked, rolling himself a cigaret. "My name's Davis. Clee Davis, *segundo* of the Rocking Chair spread." He extended a bony calloused hand. Wondering, the newcomer took it in a firm grip.

"Day is my name," he said. "Sometimes called Happy for short."

"Happy Day!" Davis grunted sourly. He cupped a match to his cigaret, the flare accentuating the thinness of his long nose, his high cheek bones and mere slit of a mouth. The quirly lighted, he moved out into the crowd. "Rider?"

"I've topped a few." Happy Day pushed out beside him.

"Bronc-peeler or cows?"

"Both." They were elbowing now, side by side, through the tight-packed mass; Happy's smoldering gray eyes still sizing up this glum-looking cowboy, who so oddly had singled him out to proffer friendship. For all the inherent suspicion of strangers in cowland he still found himself drawn to the fellow. Certainly not by his homely countenance although, Happy chuckled to himself, this stranger was too innocently homely to be very harmful.

"The Old Man, Chris Nathan, might take on a hand," the puncher offered guardedly. "But—"

Happy waited a minute, pondering the hesitation.

"Yeah," he prompted.

"It wouldn't be an easy berth."

"No riding job is."

"But this one in particular . . ."

"Wild Onion spread?"

"Finest outfit ever a man threw a leg over a bronc for—but Ed Jackson, the jasper you just busted hell out of up to the Double Eagle, is foreman."

Happy Day jerked with muscular violence. His lips pursed in a thin grim line across even teeth. He was conscious of the cowboy's gaze boring at him through the wan light.

"I'm not gunning for trouble," he said quietly. "Nor quitting the flats to get away from any either."

"That's what I thought." There was a peculiar elation in the gaunt puncher's tone. "The Old Man will be in town in the morning. If you'd be wanting to sign up . . . But don't do anything against your judgment. Don't get it into your head for a minute that Ed Jackson isn't tough; that he won't get even. . . . But you're slung about right to hold your own."

"I read his brand the minute I laid eyes on him," Happy clipped out. "Tough—just plenty—"

"Where you putting up?" Davis cut in to change the subject as they came to a stop at the end of the boardwalk, down which Happy had walked alone before the encounter in the saloon.

"Nowhere." The church spire again loomed above him in the darkness. "Figured on getting a room at the hotel for a change."

"You couldn't buy standing room with this crowd in town. Got a bed-roll?"

"Packed in."

"I'm bedding down yonder." He motioned off the single street. "Below the stockyards. There's plenty of room for another roll."

Another time Happy would have refused. But there was something real, something that rang true about this lanky puncher. And, youth though he was, Happy knew something of men.

"I'll drill back up to the livery barn and get my bed-roll," he said.

"No hurry. It's early yet; suppose we mill for a

while." Davis glanced across the street. "Believe in fortune-tellers?"

"Never met up with one."

"There's a good one here." Davis jerked a long thumb toward a booth which they were passing and around which a bunch of punchers was clustered. "She reads things in your fist . . . palm."

"Dirt's all she'd find in mine." Happy grinned. "But let's look her over if you feel lucky."

They quit the boardwalk. Happy was conscious of his new-found companion's piercing gaze. His owlish eyes were scrutinizing him, studying him, seemingly trying to pierce beyond and read his thoughts.

Side by side they elbowed through the crowd to the booth and halted on the inner rim of the crowd. A bull-necked puncher, clad in screaming shirt and flashy trappings, was standing awkwardly before them. A girl was bending over his calloused palm, while the crowd hooted and taunted him. But Happy's interest was not in the puncher. It was in the girl, although all he could see of her was a mass of fluffy hair that glistened like spun gold in the flickering light.

At that moment she looked up. For an instant their eyes met. Hers were deeply blue, Happy noticed, almost violet. Her features were lovely and glowed with healthy color, her brows were finely arched. He wished that—

But he had no time for thought. Before he could utter a protest, the girl had reached over and seized his hand. Then he stood, ears burning, a dull flush setting his face afire before the taunting crowd. She was speaking to him in a low and pleasantly husky voice.

"You're a stranger in Halfway," he heard her saying above the pounding of his own blood in his ears. "You've got a long life-line. . . . I can see a girl . . . just one. She's . . . But there is a dark man . . . Look out for him. . . . He's coming into your life to harm you."

Happy tried awkwardly to pull his hand away. The straining crowd had wedged in close beside him. Davis, at his elbow, was hanging onto every word the girl uttered.

"Watch every move you make." She was cautioning now in almost a whisper. "Always be on the lookout for that dark man."

The embarrassed Happy opened his mouth to speak. But she had dropped his hand. With only a passing glance and a friendly smile on her dainty lips she seized up the hand of a puncher next to him.

"How much?" Happy managed to blurt out.

"Twenty-five cents." The girl gave him another dazzling smile that set Happy to gulping. He drew forth the coin and handed it over to her. Then with Davis grumbling at his heels he plowed back through the crowd.

"She tipped you off," Davis said as they fell in side by side. "That girl is pulling some good stuff. Better—"

"Hell," Happy snorted disgustedly. "Do you believe that kind of chuckwallow?"

"I've got a hunch. . . ." Davis began.

"Let's bed down." Happy cut him short.

Silence fell between them as they jostled along. Reaching the stable, presently, they secured Happy's bed-roll. He hoisted it onto his shoulder. The lanky puncher leading the way, they plodded along to the end of the boardwalk. Then they took the dim trail into the darkness. After an infinity of time they reached a spot below the stockyards.

"Here," Davis grunted.

Happy dropped the tarp from his shoulder.

"I'm sure ready," he said. Unrolling his bed, he dragged off his chaps and overalls, placed his belt and gun under his pillow.

"Good night, jasper," he breathed as he passed into a deep slumber.

CHAPTER III

Dawn firing the rim of the prairies with vivid color awakened Happy Day. He lay for a time watching daylight rout the shadows about him, send them racing away through the thickets of greasewood and sage that sprinkled the valley floor. The bluffs reflected the shifting panorama of light in the east. Fire yellow flashed on yellow buttes; red sandstone took on a deeper tint in the crimson glow; cap-rock glared chalk-white. The blues and greens and slate of clays became a soft and confused mass of color. Even the drab gray of gumbo seemed to lose its ugliness in the amethyst haze that was settling down into the valley.

Above towered the Bear Lodge, somber, foreboding, black in their blanket of pine, their spiked helms aflame in the bursting day.

Happy turned on his elbow presently. Clee Davis, his new-found companion, was snoring raucously, long, peaked face screwed up mournfully.

"Daylight's burning," Happy shouted.

One of Davis's eyes squinted open. He shook himself like a wet dog, sat bolt upright to stretch.

They rolled out of their tarp beds. Quickly they pulled on their overalls and tugged on dew-damp boots. Arising, they buckled on their chaps. From beneath the soogins at their heads—where they had served as pillows—both secured their cartridge belts and holstered forty-fives.

"We oughtn't to have slept so late," Clee Davis growled in his peculiar nasal voice. "The Old Man will be in early. With daylight though, I'm almost sorry I asked you to hang around."

"Why?" Happy yawned, stretched sleepily and fell to fixing his bed-roll.

"Can't get what that fortune-teller said about a dark man off my mind. I've got a hunch—"

"Damn hunches," Happy grunted. "What's that girl's name?"

"Burton," Davis answered. "Miss Goldie Burton."

"Goldie Burton? Follow the carnival?"

Again he was conscious of the puncher's piercing gaze that he found so strange. "Reckon so. Leastwise . . . Let's eat."

Jerking the rope tight about his bed-roll, Davis straightened up. He twisted a cigaret; passed over the makin's and started away in long-legged strides toward the village, Happy, twisting a quirly as he went, at his side.

The street was almost deserted in the flush of dawn. But ample evidence of the hilarious night before lay at every hand. Banked along the rickety walks were punchers, who, either too drunk or too weary to seek their bed-rolls, had bedded down in the most convenient spot and were snoring peacefully, oblivious to the glare of the young sun that now had climbed up to tip the horizon. At the first saloon Davis stopped.

"Let's eat," he repeated gruffly.

"What's the matter with that place where I ate last night?" Happy asked. "They had good ham and eggs. Cooked right."

"The Rocking Chair gang is probably still up there," Davis offered quickly. "Jackson will still be drunk or have a hangover. . . . He'll be meaner than a teased rattler."

"That won't keep me from having just plenty of breakfast," Happy snorted.

"There isn't any use of going up there just to start a rumpus." Davis protested mildly. "I've got a hunch. . . ." There was something so doleful in his expression that Happy smiled.

"Mournful!" he exclaimed. "That's it, Mournful Davis, the man with hunches. You're Mournful Davis from now on."

"Suit yourself," the puncher growled. "But these hunches might not be so funny. We'll go to the Double Eagle if you can't eat ham and eggs anywhere else—I'm telling you though—"

Happy gave him no chance to finish. Turning on his heel, he stalked on. Mournful quickly overtook him. They strode along without speaking, their spur rowels tinkling, their high-heeled boots clamping on the hollow walk.

But apparently there were many still making merry in the Double Eagle, for as they approached they caught shouts and maudlin snatches of song.

"Still raising hell," Mournful said solemnly. "I'd feel a heap better with my stomach full, but—"

At that moment a group of punchers staggered from the saloon. Just ready to enter Happy stepped aside for them to pass. One leaped out of the gang to plant himself squarely in the path. A great fist lashed out. Happy saw it coming. Quick as the thing happened he recognized the fellow—Ed Jackson, his opponent of the night before. He tried to jerk back. But not in time. The great fist clipped him on the jaw, set his faculties to reeling.

Mournful had sprung forward. "You Rocking Chair jaspers take a sneak," he was howling. "Hunt cover . . . Every damned mother's son of you or you'll all be on the scout for a job. I'm telling you," as the bleary-eyed punchers hesitated. "Get the hell out of here!" Out of a fog of near insensibility Happy saw his long, peaked face, livid with anger. The punchers slunk back from Davis's blazing wrath. He whirled about to face Jackson.

"You're on probation at the Rocking Chair, Jackson," he almost whined in a tone that sawed on Happy's jumping nerves. "The Old Man will be in town this morning—"

"This jasper busted me," Jackson was bawling in maudlin fury. "Damn his soul, no walloper can . . ." His great hand flashed down and up. A shot crashed the quiet of the sleeping village. A slicing pain ripped across Happy's arm. He spun about, threw out his hands to keep from falling. He managed to stay on his feet, lurched into the middle of the street to stand for a moment blinking in the glare of the sun which suddenly seemed to have become a ball of fire on the rim of the valley. The brilliant light set his head to spinning faster. Pains stabbed at his eyes, raced through his head. He was panting, fighting desperately for breath, trying to find his gun but he seemed to have lost all control over his logy muscles.

The report of Jackson's gun brought the sleeping town tumbling into the street. Shouts and cries arose. Happy heard them. But they quickly died to mere whispers. The street itself took to pitching crazily. The excruciating pain in his arm centered in one black terrifying moment. He was vaguely conscious of spinning about, fists clenched, fighting, fighting to keep from going down.

Then suddenly his brain cleared. The pain subsided to a throbbing in his arm. He was vaguely conscious that the cessation of shouts had been no part of the chimera of near insensibility. He shook the haze from his eyes. On either side of the street men were lined; nerve-taut men, motionless and staring as the gaunt, weather-beaten buildings themselves.

Somewhere in the crowd he could hear Mournful cursing savagely, brutally. But he gave no heed. Before him stood Ed Jackson, thin blue smoke wreathing about his ugly livid face from the hot-barreled forty-five clutched in his hand.

Minutes dragged by; poignant, nerve-wracking minutes that were eternities. The two faced each other without moving. From the corner of his eyes, which now burned into Jackson's, Happy could glimpse chalk-white faces lining the street, chalk-white faces pressed against window panes. But the street in which they stood was clear—an open lane for swift and tragic death.

Suddenly the blinding sun made Jackson aware of its intensity. With a savage shake of his head he threw off trickles of sweat that had started coursing across his leathery cheeks. Happy smiled; a cold, lifeless smile, but remained motionless as stone; motionless save for his flame-laced eyes which looked and saw red in the brazen glare.

A gust of wind-chased spirals of dust down the street enveloped them. Sheltered for an instant behind the opaque curtain Happy's hand flashed down—a movement swift as a flutter of light. Two Colts spat flame.

Ed Jackson's knees sagged. But only for a

moment. Then he jerked straight, blood trickling from a tiny hole in the sleeve of his shirt.

Happy advanced a step, his brain now vividly clear, lightning fast. His face was marble-like in its immobility as he came on, half-crouched against the swirling dust, taut body bent like a catamount ready to spring, gun pressed tightly against his hip. No longer was it the Happy Day with the face of a youth. It was a grim-visaged Happy with hard, cruel lines at the corners of his thin lips, a deadly fearless machine. The lull, crowded with deadly expectancy, seemed unbearable. Mournful's warning recurred to Happy. The puncher had judged Ed Jackson well. For Jackson was tough—a man with nerves of iron, recklessly courageous—

The Rocking Chair foreman fired again. But now pain destroyed his aim. The bullet whined past Happy's ear. The song of hate it sang turned his soul to ice. On he came, step by step. Two shots cracked out—so close together they seemed one. Happy swayed uncertainly in the breeze. Yet his movement might have been the jerk of violently straining muscles. The tense watchers held their breath, waiting for him to go down. Still he came on.

Jackson now had stopped dead in his tracks. His Colt wavered, sunk down in fingers that could not lift its weight. His eyes were glassy, his face expressionless. He was going out on his feet, blood oozing from a second hole in the sleeve of his shirt, spreading swiftly down his arm. Then of a sudden he sat flat down on the ground, wilting slowly.

"Kill him! You've got him down now. Kill the Rocking Chair . . ."

Happy whirled. A violent curse flew to his lips. He managed to bite it back. The blazing scorn in his eyes sent the speaker slinking away through the crowd.

Happy stood for a moment as though transfixed. Then with unsteady fingers he replaced his Colt in its holster. The pain ripped back through his arm. He took a faltering step. His own knees buckled. He sprawled headlong into the dusty street.

CHAPTER IV

Happy's first conscious thought was of someone stirring above him. For a considerable time he lay struggling to overcome a terrific pounding in his ears. His head was spinning dizzily. He fought against an overwhelming nausea.

When he felt able he opened his eyes to look up into those of a girl. Out of his hazy memory he tried to place her. The infernal roaring in his head defied all effort at thought. He only knew that he had seen her. . . . That she was vaguely familiar . . . The pains shooting through his eyes forced them shut. He waited a few moments. Then he heard voices.

"He's coming to, now," came one which he somehow hazily connected with the lanky puncher. Mournful he had nicknamed him. He tried to smile. His lips felt frozen, numb. But sound of the cowboy's whining voice brought the whole affair rushing back to him with startling vividness—the battle in the street; Ed Jackson wilting, going down; the taunt from the crowd to kill him. Hot anger surged up within him, as it had done in the street. He opened his eyes again. This time to meet those of the girl above him.

"That's better," he heard a low musical voice. "Don't try things too fast now. Take it easy."

Not until then did he recognize her. It was the fortune-teller from the carnival booth in the street. The golden-haired girl with the violet eyes who had warned him to look out for a dark man. He almost expected her to say "I told you so." For all his aches the thought set the ghost of a smile tugging at the corners of his lifeless lips.

"I passed out, I reckon," he gasped out, amazed at his weakness, only half conscious of what he was saying. "Where am I?" The effort consumed him. He closed his eyes, panting. He attempted to ease an arm which felt numb and dead at his side. But to his amazement he could not.

"You're in the Halfway hotel. But take it easy." It was the voice of the girl again, scarcely audible above the roar in his ears. "Rest is what you need." She placed a damp cloth over his head, leaned over to hold its cooling folds against his throbbing temples. In spite of his dizziness and the sluicing roar of the feverish blood which nauseated him, he tingled to the pressure of her fingers.

"I'm all right," he protested weakly. "I'll just go on down and get my bed-roll—"

"You'll play the devil." It was Mournful's solemn tone now. "Your bed-roll is taken care of. And you'll lay right here and rest till you're able to move. You're shot through the arm but you'll be fit as a fiddle in a day or two. Just had Doc strap it up so you couldn't get too foxy all of a sudden."

"But Jackson," Happy managed to get out. "Is he . . . Did I . . ."

"That coyote is too ornery to kill, if that's what you're driving at," Mournful grunted sourly. "You plugged him twice through the arm—the sneaking coward. I didn't figure—"

"He shot me while I was out on my feet from that punch. . . ." A grim set came to Happy's parched white lips. "But it was my own fault. . . . Next time . . ."

"I told you Jackson was tough and dirty," Mournful growled. "But you—"

"You don't need to offer any apologies," the girl put in. "If you had—"

"Listened to what you had to say about a dark man I suppose?" Happy again attempted a smile that failed utterly.

"No," she flashed sharply. "If you hadn't fought the doctor off so hard you wouldn't have been so weak from loss of blood."

"But how, where . . ." For all her restraining hands, Happy brushed aside the cloth and sat bolt upright to stare about him. He was undressed, stretched in a real bed. A coal oil lamp, turned low, was flickering on a table beside him. A soft breeze played through open, lace-curtained windows, beyond which he glimpsed twinkling stars. He could hear the shouts of Halfway, again making merry.

"Have I . . ." he demanded huskily. "Have I been out all day?"

"You sure have," Mournful said, coming over to force him back down gently. "But Jackson hasn't come to yet. That makes a horse of him. You take it easy."

"But how—" Happy's gaze roved about the shadowed room. The plaster was cracked; faded pictures in broken frames hung from the walls; the paint was chipped from the foot of the iron bedstead.

"If you'll shut up and be quiet I'll tell you," Mournful was saying testily. "When you went down in front of the Double Eagle I was trying to hold the Rocking Chair punchers back. They were all liquored up and snorting for trouble. I didn't dare let them get loose in the street. Part of them were for Ed Jackson. The rest would have been with you. It just meant all hell. I had to let you fight it out. Sent a man hot-footing it after the sheriff. He'd left town. There wasn't anything to do but—"

"There wasn't a thing anyone would do." Happy's tone was grim and frozen. "It was a showdown that had to come sooner or later—"

"I've got a hunch it hasn't come yet," Mournful assured him sourly. "But after you went down, the Rocking Chair punchers brought you and

Jackson over here to the hotel. Both of you out cold as the fifth ace in a cold deck. I wrangled up Doc. He took care of Ed first, him being the worst shot up. Then he fixed you; but it took the whole crew to hold you down. What the devil were you fighting us for?"

"I didn't know I was," Happy said sheepishly. "But . . ." His blood-shot eyes had wandered over to come to rest on the girl, who stood looking down on him, a strange and motherly light in her violet eyes. He felt instinctively drawn to her, was conscious of a strange emotion which left him muddled.

"I called Miss Burton in—her being the only woman I knew in Halfway that I figured could—" Mournful answered the question Happy's eyes framed.

"And now that you're all right I'll be going," the girl said. "I'm glad that . . ." She laid a cool hand over Happy's. "Good-by."

Before he realized what he was doing he was gripping her hand. "I'm thanking you, Miss, for what you've done," he blurted out, ashamed of his show of feeling. "And I'm hoping that I can repay it. Even if I do have to look out for a dark man the rest of my life." He attempted to speak lightly.

But the eyes that met his frankly were heavy with seriousness. "I'm still saying it would be best for you." With that she was gone, leaving him staring at the door she had closed softly behind her.

"That was danged white of her to play mother this way to a stranger," Happy said musingly. "And it's white of you, too, Mournful."

"I'd do the same for any puncher," the cowboy grunted.

"But me being a stranger; not even belonging to the Rocking Chair spread—"

"That's where you're dead wrong," Mournful said quickly. "I signed you up the minute I read your brand last night. I saw you were righter than a rabbit. The only reason I didn't tell you was—"

"Yeah." It was Happy of old now that he had gotten control of his spinning head; the old Happy, thrifty of speech, non-committal, apparently carelessly indifferent to everything about him. Already he was censuring himself for having said too much.

"I figured you and Ed Jackson would tie up before you left town," Mournful went on presently. "And I figured that . . ."

"I wouldn't be in much shape to take a riding job."

"You're the only jasper Ed Jackson has ever tied up with in Halfway who will take a riding job," Mournful threw back significantly.

"He'll probably have something to say about me taking that job," Happy said. "He's still foreman of the outfit."

"He don't happen to be foreman when he's laid up with a couple of bullet holes through his arm." Mournful shot out. "One that will put him out of commission for a month. Me being the *segundo*, I just took the liberty of hiring you. Thirty a month and your keep—straight riding. Got the guts to take it?"

"Guts?"

"The Old Man came into town just after you had put Jackson down in the street. Yelled his head off about the way Jackson has acted up lately. He backed me up the minute I told him I'd hired you. Of course, it won't be so pleasant for you having Jackson to work under; but I've got a hunch—"

"Another one?" Happy snorted. "Where's the Old Man now? As far as Jackson being my boss . . . I'm still whole." He tried gingerly to move his numb arm. "Outside of a crippled wing," he finished grimly.

"The Old Man's . . ." Mournful almost sputtered, Happy could have sworn. "You see, he's got a fine team in here. . . . And a right smart buggy. He just took Goldie—Miss Burton out for a ride. He'll be coming along after a while. And he's taking you out to the ranch. I'm bringing your horses along for you."

Silence fell between them. Happy closed his aching eyes, suddenly prey to an overwhelming emotion; a feeling that there was more than friendship in the proffered hand that the lanky puncher had offered him the night before. The thought seemed to ease his riotous feelings, lessen the pain of his throbbing head. Presently he fell into a gentle restful sleep. Mournful tiptoed out.

It was broad daylight when Happy awoke. Again he lay for a moment trying to get his bearings. But now the sound of a voice brought him bolt upright in bed. His face lighted at sight of Mournful's gloomy features. Then his gaze flashed on to the man behind. He started. It was the grizzled old man who had directed him to the Halfway trail, who was offering his hand.

"Well, stranger," the old fellow was saying. "I tried to get you to turn back, if you'll recall. Told you this was a bad layout in here . . . But as long as you came . . ."

"You're Chris Nathan, owner of the Rocking Chair?" Happy gasped out. "And the way you were talking I thought—"

"Thinking sometimes is plumb unhealthy." The old man smiled. "But we're getting ready to move you. Doc says it's okay. Here, Davis, lend a hand."

Quickly the two raised Happy, set about dressing him. This done, they helped him up. Once on his feet he felt only a slight shakiness. In a few minutes he was able to walk without the support of either. Together they passed out of the room, down a long hallway and into the lobby.

The girl arose from one of the battered chairs in the poorly furnished room. "I'm sure glad to see you about." There was real pleasure in her musical voice that stirred Happy strangely. Her eyes were smiling in a friendly way that warmed his heart.

"But didn't you work last night," he blurted out, suddenly embarrassed and at a loss for something better to say. "Isn't it kind of early for you?"

"I got up to see you off," she said. "Is there anything wrong with that?"

She met his gaze defiantly. That look brought the strange sensation over him again. "No, I reckon not," he admitted. "And I think it is danged nice."

"I knew you would," she said, extending her hand. "Good-by."

"Good-by," he muttered, gripping her hand hard, and stalking through the door where the Old Man already was waiting in a buckboard hitched to a team of nervous broncs. Climbing in with the assistance of Mournful, he settled himself. Then he extended his hand.

"Thanks, Mournful," he said in a voice that vibrated huskily, gave the lie to the flint-hard gray eyes.

"Mournful!" the Old Man exploded.

"The kid tacked it onto me," Davis said sourly, grasping Happy's hand.

"It sure fits," the Old Man chuckled. "And I reckon it'll stick with you to your dying day. So-long, Mournful!" He shook out the reins. The broncs lunged away. Happy looked back. The girl and Mournful stood in front of the hotel watching after them.

CHAPTER V

A considerable part of the ride to the Rocking Chair ranch, far back in the Bear Lodge, was made in silence broken only by the rhythmic thud of hoof-beats and the clatter of wheels on the rutty, rain-washed road, which was little more than parallel cowtrails. The jolting of the buckboard kept Happy busy trying to protect his throbbing arm. Again he was forced to hang on grimly as the green broncs raced along, the Old Man, with spur rowels hooked under the seat, constantly flapping the reins across their backs and flicking them with a buggy whip when they showed signs of slackening the grueling pace to blow.

From time to time Happy was conscious of the rancher's inquisitive gaze upon him. But he gave no heed, content with the silence. The new surroundings, the swift pace seemed to ease the tumult of his jumbled thoughts.

After an infinity of time the road veered off around the base of a barren, ugly peak, one side of which was littered with rock splintered from a sheer face at its spiked helm. Far behind now lay the village, a bundle of buildings, dancing, swaying like a mirage in the heat. Ahead the prairie stretched endlessly, clotted with sage, gashed with flood washes. Willows traced the twisting course of creek beds, a touch of color in a vista gray and buff—a vast sweep that ended only in the purple haze where sky and prairie met.

Another sharp turn and they started into the mountains. The going became more difficult as the road wound upward, presently to become a mere scratch in the side walls of peaks that rose above them, somber, almost foreboding in their thick stand of Norway pine.

The horses now bathed in sweat had slowed down to a walk and were lunging into the collars to haul the weight of the buckboard along the boulder-littered mountain grades.

The sun climbing lazily overhead, beat down blisteringly.

"Hot!" Nathan broke the silence, lifted his hat to mop a dripping brow with a red bandana he snaked from a hip pocket.

"Sure is." Happy pulled his own hat lower to protect his aching eyes from the glare of rocks that shone like upturned mirrors in the blasting sun.

"Davis tells me you draw a pretty slick gun." The rancher jerked up the broncs just in time to keep them from plunging off the steep trail in their attempt to avoid a boulder.

"Nothing to brag about."

"Nor anything to be sorry about either in these

parts." Nathan found his plug of tobacco, deftly pared himself a slice, ground it in his hands and lighted his pipe with the same methodical slowness that Happy had noted the day they had met. "Especially when you're working under Ed Jackson as foreman."

Happy was fully aware that the wily old fellow was noting every reaction. But not by the flicker of an eyelash did he betray the slightest outward sign of what he felt.

"I'm not looking for trouble," he said shortly.

"Nor running away from any." The tone brought Happy's gaze about. But the old fellow's face was guileless as he sucked on his pipe until he had a cloud of rank smoke curling upwards.

"No." Happy's eyes snapped back to devour the majesty of the vista spread out before them.

"You a rider?" The rancher's eyes were straight ahead on the dangerous trail.

"I've ridden considerable."

Nathan regarded him quizzically for a full moment. Then he removed his pipe and chuckled. "I like you, young fellow," he said admiringly. "You can keep your mouth shut just like nobody's business. You can say plenty when you have to; and I haven't found a braggy thing about you."

"I'm just a cowhand."

"There are lots worse jobs than that," Nathan observed musingly. "The right kind of a cowhand, who buckles down to his work and uses plain everyday horse sense usually becomes a partner in a big spread. Then, some day he owns it."

Happy let the observation pass in silence.

"I could boost the wage ante ten dollars a month for a bronc-peeler," the rancher ventured shrewdly. "One who could take over the work of breaking out a rough string for a cattle drive I'm figuring on making way up on Powder River in Wyoming in about a month. Care anything about taking a whirl at it?"

"Same country you lost that thousand head in, you was telling me about the day I came?"

"Yes, but . . . It's my summer range."

"Hell for punishment, ain't you," was Happy's laconic comment. "But this job . . . What's the matter with Jackson?"

"Ed's best days are over, specially when it comes to bronc-peeling. Besides, he abuses stock. I haven't any time for a man who abuses a horse."

"I'll take your bronc-peeling job. Forty a month and all found. What do you expect?"

"I've got a pretty good string of riders." There was something of elation in Nathan's voice. "What they need is somebody to watch them; somebody to tromp them down when they get rough. I want those horses broken out so they won't be outlaws. I want stuff . . ."

"I never abuse a horse."

"You're hired." The Old Man clucked, flicked

the whip at the now leg-weary broncs, roused them from the snail pace into which they had fallen.

Again silence fell between the two. The blazing sun dragged across the zenith, starting its downward course. The shadows began to lengthen in the Bear Lodge. Purple light filtered through the timber to lie in lacy patches beneath the pines. With a lunge the broncs reached the summit. Nathan pulled rein, pointed with his whip.

"That's the Rocking Chair," he said, a note of pride in his voice.

Below, set in a wide green cañon, was a miniature city of huddled buildings, sharp-etched in the blasting sun. The side walls of the cañon rose up steeply to a crown of multi-colored gyp-rock. It was a pretty sight, an ideal location for a ranch and Happy's heart warmed to the scene.

The trip down into the cañon was made at breathless, breakneck speed. Then they were inside of wire. Punchers met them as they drove up. Some of the faces Happy recognized as having been in the crowd at the Double Eagle. They eyed him suspiciously as he climbed over the wheel. The Old Man got down. Their air of deference showed plainly the great respect in which they held him.

"This is Happy Day," Nathan said. "He's taking charge of breaking out those rough strings.

There's to be no more horses abused. He's got orders to work over the first jasper who looks cross-eyed—with a neck-yoke if he has to."

The words brought smiles to the faces of the men. One by one they advanced to shake Happy's good hand. Their clasps, he noticed, were firm and friendly. And he warmed to the crew.

The first week on the big Rocking Chair passed quickly for Happy. For all his gruff exterior, he found the Old Man amazingly solicitous of the welfare and comfort of his men. For that reason, on strict orders from Nathan himself, Happy did little work until his arm had healed completely. Never an idler, he found plenty to keep him busy, although he was careful to do it when he was certain the Old Man was nowhere about.

In his quiet, taciturn way he offered no comment at first sight of the rough string he was to supervise in breaking out. But he sized the brutes up with a practised, critical eye. Great broad-chested animals they were, weighing well above half a ton—a half ton of hell and brawn that had never been inside a corral nor felt the sting of rope. Outlaws of the worst type, they possessed the power to test the mettle of the best bronc-peeler. But the men he found were capable riders and, for all Nathan had intimated, surprisingly easy on the horses they broke out. This fact led Happy to suspect that some other motive had prompted the Old Man to employ him as a straw boss of this particular work on the Rocking Chair. But what that work was he could not for the life of him figure out.

He set to work with a grim determination to round out a string that Nathan would be proud of. Even though the rancher would not hear to him riding until he was sure of his arm, the crack of each dawn found him rolling out with the hands to pull on dew-damp boots and go yawning to the corrals for the chores.

Prairie man that he plainly was, he never failed to thrill to the dawn of the mountains; first a pale gray light, then a flash of yellow, red, orange; a shifting riot of color as the day broke over the rim-rock. Even after the infant sun had fired the gigantic pine on the helms of the surrounding peaks, the shadows lay long and somber in the yards, creeping on and on until finally the sun burst in a blinding ball through the timber. Dusk or dawn, daylight or dark, the peaks loomed directly above, gigantic sinister piles. Never did Happy tire of watching them, constantly changing, unreal phantoms . . . Now they were gray, cold, austere. Now they swayed like a gargantuan object of a nightmare in the haze, their timbered sides radiating heat like the top of a griddle-hot stove.

In its fairyland setting, the ranch itself was little less interesting. The buildings themselves were well kept; a two-story log ranch-house chinked with cement instead of 'dobe; peeled pine pole corrals; low-eaved barns built to stable countless numbers of horses. The bunkhouses were a picture as they snuggled in the cañon studded with sage and greasewood, gashed by a tiny stream. In front and behind the buildings, some half a mile, the cañon walls of multi-colored clays rose to a cap of rim-rock—greens, yellows, browns, red—a confusion of color.

The first day after his arrival had been a test that drove Happy to the limit. Most of them had seen him in action against Ed Jackson and knew that he would fight at the drop of a hat. That the others had heard about the fight and the gunplay in Halfway was evident. Yet the men had held back, waiting, watching, seeking some loophole of weakness that eventually would offer an opening to give them the edge. But Happy knew punchers; knew that tough as they were on the Rocking Chair they were amenable to reason and loyal to the boss who could command their respect. He set himself doggedly to the task at hand. Twelve hours later, by the furtive glances he drew, he knew he had won. The men, too, realized that in the thin-lipped, taciturn cowboy, the Old Man had brought out from town, they had met their master. He gave orders but once, in a low voice. Those orders, they discovered, were never repeated. Something in the way they were snapped out, the command in the cool gray eyes got action, swift and without question.

In a very few days Happy came to know his men; came to pick the friends who found companionship in his long silences and sharp-clipped conversation; came to weed out the untrustworthy, those with whom he knew sooner or later he would be forced to a showdown. A paltry few of the dozen or more riders he found to be admirers of Ed Jackson. The rest bore a smoldering hatred toward the foreman. These acknowledged Happy's two victories over Jackson by mute but loyal alliance.

Mournful had followed them out from town with Happy's mount and pack-horse. From the outset the *segundo* showed his friendship. Yet, Happy was quick to note, the crew was not particularly fond of the dour-faced puncher. For that reason he attempted to refrain from using the nickname Mournful, which he had coined. But the Old Man himself spread it among the hands. Davis instantly became Mournful to everyone. If he minded, he gave no evidence of it. He did his work in a glum sort of way. But that work was thorough, although from the start Happy sensed that Mournful's job as *segundo* was something out of the ordinary, for the lanky puncher seemed to be an especial favorite of the Old Man, with whom he spent considerable of his time.

Happy also was conscious of an unrest, a

feeling of insecurity that he could scarcely define. Through conversation with the punchers he succeeded in ferreting it out. The thing traced back to the mysterious murder of Jack Halliday, the former foreman. With the reward notice for the arrest of the assassin posted about the country, every man on the silent trails was striving to pierce the mystery, the while they were fearful that the grim unknown killer would strike again. Happy was amazed at the loyalty the crew showed for the murdered foreman. Many of them he found keeping a daily lookout for some clue that would lead to the gunman who had dropped Halliday from ambush a scant mile from the Rocking Chair ranch-house. He quizzed them quietly about the case. Yet he found that they knew little or nothing that would offer any assistance in solving the cold-blooded murder.

The Old Man's reference, the day they had met, concerning his resemblance to Jack Halliday had never been repeated. Happy himself was content to let the matter drop. And apparently the Old Man had seen something about Happy that none of the rest noticed.

May burned itself out in twisting winds that moaned in the gigantic pine and turned the green carpet to buff. The snow that had seamed the gashes in the higher peaks disappeared. The bog-holes that lined the streams down the valley turned to mud-curled patches.

June came in on a gust of sickening wind that roared constantly in the high timber; an eerie, sinister sound along with a sun that blazed down relentlessly day after day from the flawless sky above. The streams became but trickles. The buff carpet of the valley turned brown. Even the sage took on a grayish hue. That blazing June sun was but a promise of greater heat that was to follow.

Unmindful of the weather, Happy went about his work of supervising the breaking out of the rough strings. One by one they handled the brutes, rode them down, crushed them until they gave up, beaten, bruised and bleeding. But two withstood the deadening assaults. One they had named "Dirty Boy" for his wicked, treacherous traits. The other Tucson Gray, a huge brute that threw the peelers as swiftly as they climbed into the saddle.

Sight of them in action keyed Happy's nerves. He grimly resolved to ride the brutes or die in the attempt.

CHAPTER VI

Then Ed Jackson came back to the Rocking Chair. He rode into the ranch just at dusk one evening in the middle of June, an arm in a sling, his leathery face set in ugly lines, his horse dripping bloody foam. The first man he encountered in the yard was Happy, just climbing down off a perch on the corrals where he had seen his bronc-peelers top off the last horse except for the outlaws Dirty Boy and Tucson Gray.

"The Old Man really did hire you, huh?" Jackson observed sneeringly. "I thought they were just talking through their hats in Halfway."

Happy jerked straight, muscles taut. Yet only the bracing of whitened lips gave evidence of the anger that boiled within him.

"Howdy, Jackson," he said civilly, starting on to join the punchers washing for supper outside the ranch-house.

"Hold on a minute." Jackson swung down, stepped in front of his horse to block the path. "I've got a few things on my chest. . . . We've had trouble. . . . We're going to have just plenty more if you stick around here. I'm telling you now . . ."

"I don't scare worth a damn!" Happy clipped

out. He fell back a pace, gray eyes laced with flame.

"And it won't be necessary for anyone to work on the Rocking Chair under such conditions." It was the sharp voice of the Old Man, who, having seen Jackson ride in, had come up quietly from the barn to overhear the conversation. "Things have been running along right smooth without you, Jackson. . . . No trouble of any kind. We're not going to start having it now.

"Get a dally on your tongue," he warned as the bristling foreman squared away, his face livid with rage. "You haven't made such a record that this spread can't get along without you. I haven't forgotten that thousand head of prime critters you lost for me last summer trailing to Powder River."

"Rustlers got that herd," Jackson bawled furiously. "Rustlers and storms and floods."

"Yeah, I know," Nathan snorted. "But there's a hell of a lot of other things. I didn't hardly expect to see you again after the fool you made of yourself in Halfway. But now you're here, we'll just show our hands all over again. You're on probation. I've stood all the domineering of men I'm going to. Day, here, is our bronc-peeler. . . . In absolute charge of all the strings. And get this straight. He stays on the Rocking Chair."

Anger had jerked the Old Man rigid, legs

spraddled wide, open hands palm down on his hips near the cartridge belt that sagged at his waist. Jackson sized him up with blood-shot eyes. What he saw held him mute. He recognized the danger signals and had good cause to remember the rancher in a fighting mood. There were still tales of Chris Nathan's prowess along the cowland trails. Time was when his gun had reaped a heavy toll of human life. That was before rheumatism had stiffened his joints and age had dimmed his sight. But there was plenty of fire left yet and men still quailed before those narrowed, blazing eyes.

A moment passed; a moment without breath or motion.

Jackson was the first to move. He spun about, seized up his mount's trailing bridle reins and stamped away toward the barn, boot heels grinding into the ground.

Without a word Happy went on to the bunkhouse where he met Mournful, who, too, had seen the foreman ride in.

"The hell has started now," the *segundo* said glumly. "I've got a hunch. . . ."

"Do more work and you won't have time for so many of those crazy hunches," Happy snapped back.

"Is that so?" Mournful retorted sullenly. "Well, I notice . . ."

But Happy had passed inside out of earshot.

• • •

The days that followed were trying ones on the Rocking Chair. The heat became insufferable, wilting man and beast. Each day was the same, a blazing sun swimming up over the peaks in a sea of metal brilliance, climbing through the sky of glittering tin, then dropping down in a blinding red ball that sprayed the timber with the glow of a gigantic forest fire. The heat that gushed from the cedar-riven pockets and ravines was a breath from a furnace. The cañon floor gave off heat like the top of a griddle-hot stove; shimmering heat that set peaks and bluffs to swaying, distorted the horizon.

As days passed the shortage of water became acute. The hot breeze that moaned and whined incessantly stirred up spirals of dust from the beds of once trickling streams. Thirst-crazed cattle pawed at sun-curled water holes or hung across the barbed-wire fences lowing piteously. Others, driven frantic by the heat and swarms of insects, sought shelter beneath the pines where they huddled, rump to rump. The raucous bawls of prowling critters, the angry roar of a brute as it ground its head savagely in the brush to rid itself of tormenting ear flies, the trumpet of a steer goaded to flight by the pests—to run frenziedly beneath the trees, ripping away limbs like a charging elephant—beat in constant echoes back and forth across the cañon.

It was a land of beauty slowly withering, dying beneath a blasting sun; the only respite the cool breezes that strayed down from the peaks with the coming of night.

Day after day the Rocking Chair punchers drooped panting in their saddles beneath that scourging sun. Nerves frayed by the blistering heat grew raw and came near to snapping under the constant abuse of Ed Jackson. From the day of his return it seemed the foreman, despite Nathan's warning, had set out deliberately to make things so unbearable that Happy would leave. He cursed and ranted, drove the men to the point of open revolt. Not content with this he seemed to delight in piling them with work that was beyond their endurance. The ugly glances that passed between them behind his back, the snarls that met his orders were evidence of a growing hatred that might momentarily leap into a livid flame of rebellion. But Jackson played his hand with wolfish cunning, cleverly enough to avoid a showdown. He knew, as well as did the punchers, that there was not one thing they could report which he could not explain away; no single incident that would goad the Old Man to loose the dormant wrath he took no pains to conceal. Jackson was simply cursing his men to top speed without allowance for the weather.

Time and again Happy was on the point of

protesting. Much as it galled he held his tongue, ignored Jackson's veiled threats, smiled off the underhanded thrusts and bided his time until a climax was forced upon him.

That climax came one evening as the bronc-peelers crawled wearily through the poles of the corrals, where they had been working patiently beneath a blistering sun to coax the edge off the green cavvy horses they already had topped off. Gone now was the banter and fun as they waited their turn at the tin wash-basin outside the ranch-house. They snarled and growled at each other; sat sullenly on their spur rowels, staring off into space. The cook's call for supper found them trooping silently into the dining room to drop down into their chairs.

Scarcely had the plates been piled high with food when the Old Man strode in.

"How much longer will the water hold out, Jackson?" he demanded.

The foreman paused with fork uplifted. "Two weeks at the best if this weather don't break."

Happy, a cowman born, made mental calculation of conditions as he too, had noted them about the pastures. Jackson's estimate was not far from right, he concluded.

"Two weeks!" the Old Man echoed. "And not a drop this side of the river. That damned near dry too . . . Leaves us only one thing to do."

"That being?" Jackson inquired.

"Move another herd onto Powder River . . . Summer range."

A sucking intake of breath around the table greeted the announcement. Happy chanced to catch Mournful's gaze fastened upon him in that strange piercing way.

"Seems to me you'd have your guts full of Powder River after losing that thousand head there last summer," one of the punchers ventured.

"It's take the risk or lose them all," the Old Man snapped. "How about the strings?" he shot at Happy.

"About half broke out from what I can see." Jackson answered the question in a sneering tone.

The scalding blood of anger went pounding through Happy's veins.

"Plumb broke, with the exception of two," he said quietly. "The boys haven't had much luck with those—"

"Leaves us two head short for a nine-horse string to the puncher," Nathan returned grumpily. "We're pulling out of here in four days' time. We'll begin cutting the critters come daylight, Jackson—another thousand head—I can figure water for the rest on the river and in the reserves. Can those two horses be tromped down in a hurry?"

"Not by petting and coaxing," Jackson put in hatefully. "There ain't a man in this country can fork Dirty Boy or Tucson Gray without—"

"I can!" Happy's overwrought nerves snapped. He started to his feet, caught himself quickly, sat back down.

"I've got fifty dollars that says you can't," Jackson flung back.

"Keep your fifty," Happy's tone was frozen. "Let's make it a real bet. I'll tromp down one of those outlaws. Now you're so damned tough, you take the other."

CHAPTER VII

A clock-tick of silence followed Happy's challenge. It jerked the punchers around the Rocking Chair table out of their lethargy of weariness, brought them bolt upright. In that challenge they saw redress for the long and merciless punishment they had endured at the hands of Jackson. In the grim-lipped, taciturn Happy they saw a champion. The fist fight, the gunplay at Halfway flashed through every mind. Happy had bested the foreman twice, the third time . . .

Mournful started to his feet, his strange gaze riveted on Happy. What he was about to say died on his lips. He sat back down. But his great owlish eyes were everywhere. The Old Man shifted nervously, slid a hand down near the holster of his Colt.

Jackson twisted uneasily under the gazes that burned down upon him. He moved in his seat, crossed chapped legs to the tinkle of spinning rowels.

"You're on, jasper," he spat out venomously. "I'll ride—"

"You'll draw for the horse." Swift amazed glances revealed Happy apparently enjoying this crisis that other men on the Rocking Chair avoided. "You'll take it and like it, fellow." His tone was cold as chipped ice. "Play we are kids and fix a couple of straws somebody—like when we used to play pussy-wants-a-corner."

Jackson started violently. The Old Man chuckled out loud, he, too, apparently enjoying the situation that shrieked of tragedy. He strode across the room, slammed into the kitchen to return shortly with two broom straws.

"The long one takes his pick of horses." Nathan offered the first draw to Happy.

"It's his funeral." Happy jerked a thumb toward the fuming Jackson.

Nathan laughed aloud. He held out the straws to Jackson. The silence that settled down was that of chambers of the dead. Furtive glances passed between the men. Crammed mouths widened into grins.

The foreman savagely jerked forth one of the straws. Whistling sighs escaped suddenly set lips. Happy drew—the long one.

"Which of those two horses is the worst?" he asked the bronc-peelers.

"Dirty Boy!" The chorus was unanimous.

"How's your arm?" he shot at Jackson.

"Plenty good."

"Then I'll take Dirty Boy," Happy said. "I've never passed the buck to a cripple yet."

"I'm not a cripple," Jackson roared. "I'll take . . ." He stopped short. A smile jerked the corners of his lips. Alongside of Dirty Boy the other outlaw, Tucson Gray was—

"Let's carry the bet on," he suggested smoothly. "The jasper who gets thrown quits the Rocking Chair—sifts dust—for keeps."

"You're on there, too, jasper," Happy flashed back. "We'll ride under regular rodeo rules. . . . Ear 'em down or handle 'em any old way alone . . . But we ride till the cows come home . . . Stick them fore and aft seven jumps, spurs sticking east and west. The jasper who even shows daylight goes on the scout for a job."

"Covered," Jackson growled.

The tension snapped. The Old Man went out chuckling. The punchers fell to eating. Again silence descended upon them. Occasionally they glanced at Happy who was outwardly the least perturbed of the crew.

Now and then he glanced up to surprise their eyes upon him. With an inward thrill he noted the sympathy, the friendship in those gazes.

The first streak of dawn over the Bear Lodge found the men rolling out of their bunks. Quickly the wranglers ran the new-broken string into the corral; Dirty Boy and Tucson Gray galloping and snorting in the lead. With a hateful glare, Jackson crawled inside, his wounded arm minus the splint. Singling Tucson from the milling mass he snapped a rope across the brute's neck and, quick as a flash, took a dally around the snubbing post.

Striking, bawling, fighting his head the sweating Jackson slowly worked the brute in.

Two lengths from the post he lunged, teeth gnashing savagely. Jackson dodged, jerked up the slack, jammed the flaring nostrils against the post. The big, dirty gray brute threw its weight on the rope. Breath began rasping in his throat. Its legs began to tremble with the violence of the resistance. Inch by inch the outlaw sank down. Presently its belly touched the ground. Then with a grunt it dropped. Choked down, it rolled onto its side.

Slipping a hackamore over the flailing head and anchoring his saddle was but a few minutes' work.

Then Jackson stood beside the outlaw, waiting for it to rise. The men leaped into the corral to pay out the rope. Tucson Gray sucked his lungs full of air, rolled over onto his belly. He came lurching to his feet. Jackson swung aboard.

For a moment the outlaw stood trembling, eyeing the punchers who had strung out along the top poles of the corrals. Then he bowed his neck, went skyward, Jackson a whipping figure on the apex of the clevis body. Tucson Gray straightened out, swapped ends, let forth a bawl and sun-fished until his belly showed in the glowing dawn. Before his feet touched the ground, he snapped about, skyrocketed into the air, reared on hind legs, swaying perilously for a moment, and somersaulted backwards.

Jackson managed to free his feet from the

stirrups, throw himself headlong from beneath the half ton bearing down upon him. The brute lit with an impact that shook the corrals. The saddle-horn snapped. The cantle flattened out. Only stunned by the fall, Jackson sprang to his feet. Quick as a flash he rolled under the bottom pole, seized up a neck-yoke and rolled back inside. He came up with the half-stunned horse, sent the neck-yoke crashing against the brute's head. It shuddered, dropped back, straightened out with a groan.

A violent oath brought Jackson spinning about. Happy had leaped into the corral, his gray eyes red in the glare of the infant sun tipping the peaks. "You—" Anger choked him. One hand went to his holster. Jackson leaped back. His own hand started down.

"Don't go for it," Happy lashed out. "Damn your soul, I ought to kill you. . . . Hitting a game-fighting horse that way. But it's like you, you yaller-livered four-flusher. . . ." At that moment Tucson Gray struggled up, went lurching toward the corral gates, which the punchers had dropped, bolted outside and trotted away.

Happy whirled on the crew. "Run Dirty Boy in," he yelled. "Let's have a clean ride! If I get dumped I'll not use a neck-yoke." He snapped around—his movement was that of a puma. "Get out of the corral," he blazed at Jackson. "You," he barked at the men above. "Get a bead on him—"

"I've got it." It was the Old Man's voice. "Ride that horse, cowboy. Jackson won't even look crooked or—"

The fuming foreman crawled outside the corral to stand watching, his back to Nathan. Never once did he turn. Neither did his hand creep toward his forty-five.

Once the bunch was back in the corral, Happy popped his noose around the neck of Dirty Boy. The big bay came back fighting with every ounce of its mighty twelve hundred pounds. . . . It struck, snorted, bellowed . . . Bared teeth clicked . . . The taut rope whined under its terrific lunges. Yet inch by inch Happy, alone now in the corral, dragged the lunging brute into the snubbing post.

Presently its flaring nostrils were jammed tight. A couple of diamond hitches made it powerless. But for all its croupily rasping breath it refused to drop. The choking brute stayed on its feet, eyes glazed, belly heaving. Then slowly the burning rope put it down. It plunged frantically. Knees buckled. Dirty Boy threw himself in a heap.

Now it was Happy saddling, talking constantly in a soothing tone to the horse. Once, as he shoved the latigo beneath the lunging brute, he caught sight of the Old Man making a threatening gesture with his gun. But whatever Ed Jackson had in mind, as he turned to cast a furtive glance behind him, was forgotten. For he brought both hands high above him to clutch the corral poles.

Then Happy called for the men. They cast loose the throw rope. Dirty Boy lurched up in a wild, unbalanced leap. A great shout arose. Happy was in the middle of him. As the brute hit the hard-packed earth, to pound up puffs of dust, Happy's rowels sunk home. They brought a bawl from the outlaw. It downed his head, pitched away, a half ton of weaving, bawling, twisting hell and brawn.

The ride Happy Day made that day is history on the Rocking Chair. He rode Dirty Boy through bone-cracking lunges, fanned him with his hat when he went sky high to come down, nose where his tail started. He yelled and he taunted, laced the brute from shoulder to rump with his rowels. Now Dirty Boy was sun-fishing, turning his belly to the sun. Now he was crouched, waltzing, springing away, front legs stiff as rails, hind legs bullfrogged, dragging.

The killing pace quickly began to tell. The brute weakened. So did Happy. But he roweled on. The Rocking Chair punchers were yelling at the top of their voices. That welter of praise came only distantly to Happy. His body felt beaten to a pulp. He was swaying in the saddle, boneless, his body whipped to a dish-rag. One jump broke the crystal of the watch in his trouser pocket. A wild, crazy leap brought the blood gushing from his nose. But he hung on grimly, stubbornly, until

Dirty Boy stopped, fore legs spraddled, trembling like those of a new-born colt.

"Drop the corral poles!" Happy jerked out.

The punchers did as they were bid. Happy roweled the half-dead brute through the gate, jerked him around the corral. A few more wild lunges and again Dirty Boy stopped, broken, bruised, bleeding.

Happy climbed down to stand swaying drunkenly. He ignored the hand of the Old Man—of Mournful, too.

"Our bet being . . ." He hurled through set teeth at Jackson. He reeled against the corral poles, braced himself a minute, swiped his eyes as though in a daze. . . . "One of us was to pull out freight. It's your move, Jackson."

"The hell it is," Jackson bawled, his fury bursting all bonds. "Damn you—"

"Hold on, Ed." The Old Man interposed. "It does mean you. You called the bet fair and square. Now you're following through. You're fired. Happy Day is the new foreman of the Rocking Chair ranch. That means from this minute on. Happy Day is the man who takes charge of that Powder River drive."

Jackson's livid face twitched convulsively. But anger choked him.

The men moved in around the Old Man.

"You've heard the orders, Jackson," Happy said quietly, standing spread-legged, his hand dangling just above the butt of his gun, that Mournful had slid into his holster. "Now you take a sneak. As foreman of this spread, I'm telling you . . . I don't want you under Rocking Chair fence after sundown."

One baleful glance at the set faces around him and Jackson spun on his heel, started toward the bunk-house.

"You've won this hand, jasper," he hurled at Happy. "But I'll win the next."

"He's won a couple of them if I recall right," Mournful taunted in a tone that brought Happy's inquisitive gaze upon him.

"But he's not through on this range by a hell of a sight," Jackson bawled. "I'm laying money—"

He got no further. Happy bounded in front of him. "Laying money on what, fellow?" he demanded quietly; so quietly that his voice was almost a purr.

Jackson jerked with violently straining muscles, passed on. A few minutes later, duffle bag rolled, he rode out of the Rocking Chair. With never a backward glance he hit the trail for Halfway in a cloud of dust.

CHAPTER VIII

The Powder River badlands lay panting beneath the blazing July sun. Heat rose in shimmering waves from the sun-baked flats. Heat gushed from deep, sheer-walled washes. Heat radiated from weirdly-shaped buttes, that reared up stark and ugly; their crumbling sides corrugated like molten metal that has burst its mold and cooled as it ran. Heat distorted the horizon, unreal, everchanging.

Sage and greasewood drooped wearily, withered, seered, dusty as the rustling grass that struggled for existence on the blistered gumbo. Here and there a cottonwood bent over a ravine, blighted and dwarfed by its long and hopeless fight for water. The breeze that whined in the coulees was breathless, stifling with the scent of hot sage and fennel.

It was a land of utter desolation, parched, thirsty, heaving beneath a sky of glaring brilliance.

Far to the west Powder River slashed the purple haze like a thread of silver, the one respite from the dead and lifeless hue of withered things. Beyond—a faint blue etching on the skyline—swayed the Big Horn mountains.

Eastward a fog of dust shortened the horizon,

rose like a pall of smoke to settle down and hang along the back trail—dust scuffed up by the big Rocking Chair herd, plodding across the humid flats toward Powder River.

Dust rimmed the sunken, glassy eyes of the brutes. Sweat moistened the base of bobbing ears. Heads pumped wearily, almost scraped the ground. Mud-caked legs moved heavily, mechanically. Heat and thirst had drawn hides taut across staring ribs; had deepened the hollows in gaunt flanks. A seemingly endless procession they moved, the rear but hazy phantoms in the murk of heat and dust.

On either side of the shuffling leaders was a point man. Wilted by the heat they rode, dozing in their sticky saddles, bridle reins hanging loose, neckerchiefs drawn up to shield the lower part of grimy faces. Flopping brims of weather-beaten hats were pulled low to protect blood-shot, aching eyes from the glare of the late afternoon sun on blinding patches of alkali and glazed rock that shone like upturned mirrors.

Strung out along the herd were the flank riders. They hunched like bullfrogs in their saddles, beaten to drowsiness by the merciless sun.

All but obscured in the dust cloud at the end of the straggling column were the tail riders, cursing and prodding the drags. Still behind them wandered the cavvy, grazing in spite of the heat under the sleepy but watchful eye of the dog-tired wrangler. The cook, fat, perspiring, panting—sprawled precariously on the bed-rolls aboard a jolting wagon—brought up the rear of the caravan.

Aside from the cowboys and the herd few living things braved the relentless heat on that vast and illimitable expanse. Now and then a startled cottontail darted to the mouth of a hide-out in the grottoed bank of a flood wash, to hunch fearfully, ears pink in the blazing sun. A sand rattler coiled to hiss a protest at the rude interruption of its lazy sunning and send a horse or steer shying. A coyote slung through the brush, paused for a surreptitious peep from the rim of a draw. A bunch of antelope—forever cutting across the path of any intruder—shot like a streak ahead, gained the opposite side to stop broadside and watch, flags bristling, glaring white. An occasional bunch of range cattle stopped grazing to throw up their heads and stare inquisitively at the invading herd, then bawl an unanswered challenge, roll their tails and bolt.

A stillness as oppressive as the heat itself lay over the desolate regions of ravines, gullies, dry washes and gumbo buttes; a stillness unbroken save for the monotonous rattle of hoofs, the click of horns, the hoarse cough of a dust-choked critter or the roar of a steer goaded to frenzy by thirst and the flies and gnats that hovered in clouds over the peeling road brands of the herd—a freshly-burned circle, or Ringbone, around the sharply-protruding right hip bones.

Where the trail wound around the base of a barren, ugly butte, then meandered off across a brush-choked alkali flat toward the rim of a deep and jagged ravine, Mournful Davis shifted sidewise in his saddle, weight in one stirrup.

"Jumpin' Jerusalem, but it's hot," he growled. "And on top of it I've got a hunch that all hell is about due to break loose."

He swiped glistening particles of alkali from the stubble on his peaked chin.

Happy Day, his companion on the point, the new trail boss of the herd on its pilgrimage to summer range on Powder River, lifted his hat to brush damp hair back from a sweat-beaded brow.

"I was just riding along here wondering how long it would be before one of your hunches would be cropping out, Mournful," he laughed. He, too, dropped the kerchief from his nose and mouth and tight-reined his horse to slap the dust from his flannel shirt. "I sure said a mouthful when I nicknamed you Mournful, didn't I?"

"You're funny, there's no doubt about it," the solemn-faced puncher returned testily after a time, in his peculiar nasal twang. "But to my way of thinking that is a heap better than what they did by you when they tacked that high-falutin' monicker onto you. Happy Day—I'd rather play one of my hunches now and then and dodge a little trouble than never to worry about anything and wait until trouble romps up and down my carcass like you do."

"You're getting worse than that fortune-telling girl in Halfway," Happy flashed. "The next thing you'll be warning me, like she did, to keep my eye peeled for a dark jasper who is coming into my life to raise twenty different kinds of merry hell." He eased his mount down into a wash, leaned forward in the saddle to distribute his weight as it scrambled up onto the other rim.

"She was giving you a straight tip," Mournful observed in a tone of judicial thought, pulling up beside him, only to draw rein and wait for the leaders to amble up to the wash. "There are two things you can bank on—fortune-tellers and my hunches."

"Specially if the fortune-teller happens to be good-looking." Happy touched his mount with the rowels and moved on as the weary cattle started up out of the wash. "Ever hear from her, Mournful?"

The gaunt puncher shot him one of those inscrutable, searching glances that Happy many times had attempted to fathom without success.

"She was mighty nice to you when you were crippled up in that shooting scrape." Mournful's tone was full of mild reproach. "Miss Burton . . ."

"She sure was." Happy fished a sack of tobacco

and papers from the pocket of his shirt, twisted a cigaret and passed over the "makin's."

"You're just sore because we had something in common." Mournful accepted the proffered smoke, measured out the tobacco in a paper, jerked the sack shut with his teeth and rolled a quirly between thumb and forefinger in a single, deft movement. Flaring matches brought snorts from suddenly roused horses.

"That being?" Happy snuffed out his match, broke it in two and tossed it into the seered brush.

"I was referring to our occult power."

"You never heard of occult power until she sprung it on you," Happy snorted. "Then you had to pump a bartender in Halfway to find out what it meant. . . . The boys told me."

"Just because I wasn't familiar with what it was I had, wasn't any sign I didn't have it," Mournful pointed out with a patient air. "I suspect I've got an appendix too. But I've never seen it. I wouldn't even know it was there if some smart jasper hadn't discovered it and told me about it. I'm chuck full of occult power. That's what gives me my hunches."

Happy regarded him quizzically for a moment. But, as usual, his doleful, mask-like expression gave no indication as to whether he was joking or was deadly serious.

For all their close association since the day of his arrival in Halfway, Mournful still remained an enigma to Happy. And to everyone else, for that matter. The *segundo*'s past was shrouded in mystery. Some said he was playing a part, his mournful mien but a mask to conceal his real character and purpose; others that beneath his outward solemnity—and sometimes almost too obvious slow wit—he was laughing at them all. No one knew. And in a land where a man's past was his own no one attempted to find out. Suffice to say that in the few months since his appearance from nowhere to take employment with the Rocking Chair spread, they had come to know him only as an expert puncher, nervy, an indefatigable worker who was suspicious of everyone and superstitious of everything; always morose and gloomy in contemplation of the calamities he imagined his occult power enabled him to foresee. He offered no friendships, received none. With one exception. That exception was Happy Day.

From the start the two had hit it off amazingly well. In spite of their peculiarly clashing personalities Happy apparently found something in the melancholy cowboy that rangeland did not. For they became inseparable companions. And of all the Rocking Chair crew Happy alone was elated when, at the last minute, the Old Man had let Mournful go on the long drive to summer range on Powder River.

"Your hunches give me a pain," Happy said

presently, squaring himself in his sticky saddle. "I kind of figured that now we've been on the trail from the last camp ten hours without water that one of them was brewing. . . . Also noticed you don't have them near so often or regular when you're doing the things you like to do—being with Miss Goldie Burton, for instance. Buck up. You'll run across her again someday."

"She isn't worrying me any," Mournful snorted disgustedly, "But the way you keep making fun of that dark man, she warned you to keep an eye peeled for, is. It's plumb dangerous, Happy, this business of ignoring hunches. Let me tell you that girl knew her P's and Q's."

"Mebbeso," Happy conceded. "But I still say there's nothing to worry about."

"Nothing to worry about?" Mournful groaned. "You, a kid, trail-bossing a thousand head of prime Rocking Chair critters that haven't had a drop of water in ten hours and sundown only a little ways off. Suppose you don't locate water tonight?" He jerked a gnarled thumb toward a mass of fluffy thunderheads climbing lazily into the sky. "This kind of heat is bound to breed weather. You don't want to forget we heard in Halfway that Ed Jackson bet a pile of money you'd never take this herd through to Powder River and bring it back."

CHAPTER IX

Mention of Ed Jackson brought Happy straight in his saddle, eyes suddenly glinting in the brazen glare.

"Damn Ed Jackson and his bets!" he exploded. "We haven't lost so much as a drag in the two weeks we've been on the trail. And we're danged near to the river right now."

"Ed Jackson never lost one of the thousand Rocking Chairs he was trail-bossing to this same range for the first two weeks he was out with them last summer either," Mournful reminded almost maliciously. "Then what happened?"

"Jackson's story of losing those critters in floods, storms and to rustlers sounds fishy to me." Happy flung back.

"The Old Man hasn't had Jackson arrested." Mournful's shrug was an insinuation that would have nettled anyone but Happy Day.

"But you'll notice he's posted a standing reward of twenty-five hundred dollars for information leading to the recovery of the herd. That ought to show how he figures. The boys say he's hired the best range detective money can get to come into the country and nose around—an old Texas ranger. He sure must be some pussyfoot for I've never seen hide nor hair of him—nor anybody else to my knowledge. Wonder where he hangs out?"

"It's Ed Jackson I'm thinking about," Mournful said shortly. "He's got just plenty to hate your guts for. It's a danged sight worse than ever now, since the Old Man fired him and gave you his job. His story about losing those critters up here in these badlands somewhere may sound fishy. But you can just bet the ace that he isn't doing all his talking through his hat—not by one devil of a ways. Ed Jackson is nobody's fool; he knows these badlands like a book. That's a danged sight more than you or I can say, this being our first trip." He shifted his weary body sidewise in his saddle, weight in one stirrup, to look back again along the line of bobbing rumps. "And there ain't a danged bit of use trying to fool ourselves. These critters weren't any too good when we started two weeks ago. . . . They're in a bad way for water now."

"They're no thirstier than I am." Happy turned to follow his gaze. "I'll live through it. It can't be far now to the river. We can crowd them through after dark if . . ."

"And lose half of them in a stampede as quick as they get a scent of water . . . The rest of them in the river," Mournful cut in to snort. "That would be a smart trick. Just the thing to win that bet for Jackson."

"Worrying about water isn't going to bring

it to us any quicker." Happy faced the blistered flats ahead. "We'll come through all right. Forget Jackson. Let him bet I'm going to lose this herd. Bellyaching isn't going to get him anywhere."

"It's this hunch I've got that we're due for a lot of trouble before we get back to the Rocking Chair home ranch," Mournful growled. "And that girl warned you—"

"You're a danged old calamity howler," Happy growled. "Ever since that girl told my fortune, sprung that dark man business, you've spent your time predicting all sorts of fool things. Dark man, hell! I've stacked up against a lot of dark men. Ed Jackson was one. And I reckon . . . You don't really believe that fortune-telling stuff, Mournful?"

"Of course I believe it," Mournful returned soberly. "And Ed Jackson might of been the jasper she was trying to warn you about for all you know. You haven't heard the last of him by a long ways. I tell you we're due for hell—just plenty of it. We—"

He broke off abruptly to draw rein on the rim of a steep wash and stand rigid in his stirrups. As though a signal, the leaders, eagerly anxious to rest, came to a halt. One by one the entire column stopped, began breaking to graze. The flank riders came to life, goaded their tired ponies along the line to turn back the brutes.

"What's eating you now?" Happy too jerked up. "Sun softening your brain?"

"There's the hell I've been feeling in my bones!" Mournful exclaimed with almost malicious glee, pointing ahead with a bony finger.

Happy strained through the shimmering heat haze for a glimpse of what his companion had seen. Far ahead, barely distinguishable in a great cloud of dust, was another herd moving down the trail toward them!

"They're going to meet us head-on!" Mournful shouted with an amazing show of spirit.

"What of it?" Happy snapped taut in his saddle. "We've met herds on the trail before. How is this one going to hurt us any worse than any of the others?"

"They'll mix from hell to breakfast with our stuff." Mournful shot a swift glance back along the herd. "It would mean holding our critters off water until we worked them and cut out all these strays."

"I wouldn't hold these critters off water for the Old Man himself!" Happy's quick decision was typical. "It will be that herd that's due for a return trip up the trail. If the wallopers driving them don't like it they'll just have to . . . These Rocking Chairs are going to water. All hell can't stop them. Your occult power didn't figure on us being able to muster ten of the best hands who ever drove cows."

"That's all right," the puncher growled, "but I still say it's a danged sight better to be ready for trouble than to—"

"Shut up!" Happy jerked about in his saddle, swept the long dusty line behind, motionless now, ears cocked forward, staring inquisitively.

"There's another herd coming fellows!" he shouted. "Two of you shag up here . . . Take our places on the point. Mournful and I will meet them. . . . Ease them by. Tight-pack our stuff. Throw them into a mill if you have to. But hold those other critters out."

Before the punchers had shaken off their lethargy and started to execute his orders, he had lifted his mount with stinging rowels and was gone over the rim of the ravine. Mournful, his dusty, wrinkled face screwed up thoughtfully, pounded after him.

Urging his blowing mount up the steep trail on the opposite side of the draw, Happy tight-reined to a running walk.

"Do you see anybody driving them critters, Mournful?" he asked, peering ahead at the herd, a mile or more distant and still obscure in the cloud of dust.

"Nope. But you can bet your sweet life somebody is, by the way they're bunched and busting the breeze—not only driving them but crowding them hard."

"It's damned strange they'd be coming along

so all-fired fast without a jasper in sight." Happy mused aloud. "Unless—"

"They're stampeding, that's what they're doing!" Mournful exclaimed. "Ten to one they've got their tails rolled. They wouldn't have if somebody was driving them. Didn't I tell you hell was going to break loose? Now give me the horse laugh, will you? These herds are going to mix as sure as the devil. For all we can do . . . And if that bunch don't stampede our stuff we'll be damned lucky!"

His words were lost to Happy who again had brought his pony to life with slashing rowels and was racing along to meet the herd thundering down the trail toward them. Once, as he held his blowing horse to a straight course over the brush-clotted ground, he glanced back to catch the eye of Mournful riding directly behind, long arms flapping like the wings of a crane.

"I told you so!" the *segundo* panted. "For God's sake don't get in the path of those brutes or you'll . . ."

Happy's answer was to spur out of hearing.

Up the trail the two raced toward the on-coming herd. The lowering sun beat down brazenly, streaking their faces with sweat and covering their tired but willing mounts with foam.

Then, like a gigantic wave, the herd burst from the enveloping cloud of dust directly in front of them. Mournful dodged to the right. Happy barely had time to drag his pony from the trail to the left as the leaders swept by, heads up, tails rolled, terrifying bawls rumbling in their throats. Setting his mount on its haunches he wheeled and started in pursuit.

After the first few minutes of the killing pace his weary pony succeeded in getting its second wind. Putting its heart and soul into the race, with a gigantic effort that drew its already gaunt flanks, it crept up. Happy tried to pierce the billows of dust for sight of Mournful. He could see nothing of him. He dared a glance over his shoulder for a glimpse of the punchers, who had the herd in charge, and who shortly must be making an appearance in an attempt to overtake it. No living thing moved behind that herd . . . only great clouds of alkali dust that were settling down in streamers along the back trail.

Digging the rowels into his horse, already nearing the limit of its strength, he closed the gap, pushed up abreast of the leaders. His mount bounced on stiffened legs to change the course of its headlong flight without losing its footing. Caught on the edge of the surging torrent, Happy barely escaped being sucked into the vortex of deadly hoofs. He gave his pony rein. Freed of the guiding hand, it managed to dodge the mass and plunge to safety.

Shaking with exertion and terror, it increased its speed. The frenzied herd thundered alongside like an angry, foaming river at flood stage, sweeping everything before it, trampling sage and greasewood, crushing down all in its path that dared defy its devastating advance. The incessant rumble of hoofs, the click of horns, the hoarse bawls that rose like the roar of a great planing mill, combined to produce a bedlam, made more horrible by the sickening heat and the clouds of choking dust that rolled skyward to settle back in dirty gray waves. It was a maddened, blinded mass, tearing across the flats; slavering brutes plunging through ravines, hurtling clumps of brush, dodging impossible jumps only to be jostled aside by their on-coming mates.

With shouts, curses and barking Colt, Happy tried to swerve the gaunt leaders, which, with tails rolled, lumbered at the head of the column. But they clung to the trail with crazed tenacity.

Before he realized it they had reached the rim of the wash across which Mournful had first sighted them. Like a gigantic cataract they poured over the bank. Happy jerked up for an instant to look for Mournful. He could see nothing through the great sheets of dust except the sea of swaying, heaving rumps. Hoping fervently that his *segundo* had not gone down, he plunged on, trusting to luck that his mount would keep its footing.

Across the floor of the ravine they fled. Ahead, Happy caught a glimpse of the Rocking

Chair herd, lined up in a solid front, staring inquisitively. His men were galloping out to meet the oncoming brutes, brandishing slickers, waving their hats. Forty-fives were cracking a staccato challenge. But their efforts to stop the rush were doomed to failure. Up the bank of the ravine bounded the bawling, slavering critters.

"Mill the Rocking Chairs! Mill our stuff!" Happy bellowed at the top of his voice. "They'll stampede too if you don't stop. . . ." His words were lost in the noise that rose in a crescendo tumult.

CHAPTER X

Unable to command his men, yet trusting to luck that they would follow any example he set, Happy raced forward at breakneck speed, leaned over in his saddle, seized the tail of a big, raw-boned Rocking Chair steer and almost threw it off its feet in a frantic attempt to start it running in a circle. The cowboys caught his meaning and followed suit. But their desperate efforts were to no avail. Before the sweating, cursing crew could start the mill the damage was done. The two herds met head-on in a choking cloud of dust. The lethargy that had gripped the Rocking Chair herd vanished magically. Instantly the wild-eyed brutes were beyond control, seemingly possessed of but one instinct—to stop the strange animals that had come thundering down the trail to do combat. Fore feet planted, heads lowered, snorts whistling through flaring nostrils, terrifying bawls rumbling in their throats, they met the onslaught.

Pandemonium broke loose. The two herds fell to fighting savagely; shoving, crowding, vicious horns lacing the air . . . Brutes went down in struggling heaps . . . Hoarse bellows of pain drowned out the shouts, curses and the roar of gunfire. The scent of blood drove the critters to a frenzy. Back and forth moved the two lines, horns locked now, straining hoofs plowing up furrows of gumbo, neither gaining, neither giving ground.

"We've got to mill them somehow," Happy thundered at the top of his voice. "Step across a steer if you have to. . . . Mill them any old way you can!"

Mournful jerked up beside him, his horse dripping lather, champing the bit nervously.

"It's too late!" he bawled. "They've already mixed. The best we can do is circle them. This here is the hell. . . ."

"Glad you came through all right," Happy panted. "But if you open your chops again about hell busting loose I'll wrap my forty-five around your head. Here you jaspers—pick yourself out a critter. . . . Step across. It's our one chance to hold 'em!"

He roweled alongside a big, raw-boned steer, leaned far over to grasp its horns like a bull-dogger, shot from his saddle onto its back, drove his rowels into its sides and began fanning it with his hat. Riderless, his pony threw up its head and, with bridle reins trailing, ran off a short distance from the melee to whirl and stare at the strange proceedings.

Happy's reckless move momentarily halted the battle. The two lines drew apart to roar bellowed challenges at one another and paw the earth, throwing up suffocating clouds of dust. Before they met in another charge Happy had spurred the terrified steer from the mass. Rolling its tail it bolted, pitching and bawling. With almost a superhuman effort he succeeded in staying on the twisting back, beat it alongside the head with his hat until he had it running in a circle.

He dared a glance over his shoulder. Led by Mournful, the other punchers had climbed aboard steers. Following his lead with the blindness of sheep, the cattle had taken to pounding on his heels. Others, seemingly anxious to be out of the choking, maddened mass, followed. Shortly the whole scene resembled a gigantic roulette wheel, the center stationary, the outer rim gyrating dizzily. One by one the leaders, deserted by their bellowing cohorts, left off their fighting to join the merry-go-round. Presently the brutes were running in a circle. But the two herds were hopelessly mixed.

Round and round went Happy, his head spinning, his body aching from the punishment inflicted by the sharp withers of the heaving brute beneath him, yet yelling like an Indian, raking the steer from shoulder to rump with bloody rowels and managing to beat it alongside the jaw with his hat. Until utter weariness forced the big animal to slow down to a lumbering trot and it began to stagger, did he stay with it. Then, when it had all but reached the point of collapse, he leaped off, dodged outside the mass and peered through the choking dust. The weaker animals had ceased their milling and were jammed in the center of the herd where they huddled in terror, attempting to escape across one another, heads thrown across each other's backs, slaver smeared sides heaving, breath rasping croupily in parched throats. Others had dropped to the ground where they lay panting, too weary to rise, or attempt to escape the sharp hoofs clipping about them. The bawling few that continued to trot in a circle were swiftly playing out.

Moving in as closely as he dared, Happy tried to read the brands on the strange animals. But apparently in the melee the newcomers had been jammed into the center for the few he was able to see, in the mass of terrified critters, that lunged wildly away at his approach, were all Rocking Chairs with the Ringbone road brand.

"I reckon there wasn't a critter killed or crippled bad in the big scrap," he muttered, moving back to a safe vantage point to survey the herd with critical eye. "Though I'll bet a good part of them have got bumps they wish they didn't have."

Skirting the edge of the bunch presently to where his pony stood, head up, ears cocked, nostrils flaring, its weariness forgotten in the terror of the moment—he stopped to sweep the murky badlands, purple in the light of late afternoon. Although a considerable time had elapsed since the strange herd first appeared, still there was no sign of the cowboys who must have had the stampeding cattle in charge—if, indeed, there had been any one with the brutes. Nothing moved on the dreary wastes that stretched away illimitably save a long, low-hanging cloud of dust that swayed gently in all directions, settling down in a thin gray film on man and beast and brush.

"If this isn't the damnedest thing I ever heard of?" he blurted out in his perplexity, check-reining his shying horse and swinging into the saddle. "Wonder who in the devil that herd belongs to?" He turned from his survey as his dust-covered punchers straggled up, coughing, cursing, mopping the sweat and grime from their faces. "Seen anything of the wallopers this herd belongs to?" he asked them.

A negative reply came from all in growls and snarls.

"Looks like a frame-up to me," volunteered Mournful, coming up to capture his horse—which snorted and shied away with devilish glee. "A dirty, lousy frame-up of some kind. I'm warning you to go easy, Happy. I've got a danged, sneaking . . ." He jerked a tight rein, swung into the saddle to snap straight and take hurried stock of the surroundings.

"If you mention a hunch to me again today I'll tromp you to death even if you are the *segundo* of this lay-out!" Happy rasped out. "Everything is a frame-up to you. Even a couple of hundred critters getting scared at their shadow up yonder somewhere and running down the trail . . . We happen to be coming along. . . . They mix with our herd. . . . That's a frame-up to your way of thinking. It could happen on any range. . . . Anytime. . . . There's nothing strange about that."

"Oh, ain't there?" Mournful shot back icily. "Nothing strange about where they came from? Or the fact that nobody has showed up to claim them? That's a pretty big bunch just to be prowling the range and stampeding for no cause at all only getting scared of their shadows, as you say. But don't overlook the fact—"

Before he could finish Happy turned away impatiently. At the moment a growl of thunder, faint with distance, drew his attention. He shot an apprehensive glance at the sky. The thunderheads had lost their fluffy whiteness, had become ugly and black, tinged with green in the setting sun.

"Storm coming," he said abruptly. "That green looks like hail."

"Oh, Lord," Mournful groaned. "I knew this weather would breed weather. . . . I . . ."

"We've got to locate water quick. . . . Bed down!" Happy gave the long-faced *segundo* no chance to finish his dire prediction. "One of you jaspers scout that up trail. Ride like the mill-tails of hell. We'll get these brutes to moving, crowd them hard. We'll go as far as we can—"

One of the crew stuck spurs to his horse, was gone in a cloud of dust. Happy stood up in his stirrups, whirled. “Prod the critters up, jaspers. Tired as they are we’ve got to shag them along unless we want to get caught in a storm.” Roweling his pony into a lope, he started around the herd, only to jerk rein at a violent oath from Mournful.

“Here comes the gang we don’t want to see right now,” the *segundo* groaned.

Happy wheeled about. His eyes whipped up the trail in the direction Davis was pointing. A group of horsemen had appeared suddenly from behind a butte.

“Now our hell is plumb complete,” Mournful moaned. “It just means holding our Rocking Chairs off of water until these critters are cut out.”

“Not by a hell of a ways it don’t!” Happy was rigid as a steel bar in his stirrups. “We didn’t pick up these strays on purpose. These gents will wait until we find water to get their cows.”

“You’re going to have to lie then,” Mournful warned.

“What about?” Happy flashed. “Why?”

“You’re going to have to tell them we haven’t seen anything of their stuff,” Mournful argued. “If you admit we’ve got them in our herd we’ll have to work ’em out. You’re not on your home range now, you know. They don’t know us. This is Powder River. . . .”

"What do you know about Powder River?" Happy demanded.

"Nothing. But I've got a hunch that—"

"Damn your hunches!" Happy's gaze flashed back to the approaching horsemen. "You might of called the turn about hell breaking loose. . . . But you're sure off your base when you think I'm going to lie about these strays being in our herd. . . . Or hold our thirsty Rocking Chairs from water for any box-kneed wallopers who haven't got sense enough to handle their own stuff. Hunches be damned. These Rocking Chairs are going to water. Prod them up, fellows!"

CHAPTER XI

With furtive glances at the horsemen, six in number, who were riding leisurely down the trail, the Rocking Chair punchers roweled away to do Happy's bidding. With shouts, kicks and curses they got the weary cattle to their feet. Satisfied that the approaching men had been in charge of the stampeding herd, but determined to brook no further delay, even if forced to compel them to follow up the trail to reclaim their brutes, Happy moved over beside Mournful and sat his mount watching them. Their apparent lack of haste puzzled him. Nor did their horses show any evidence of the grueling run they must have made before the herd broke away from them completely.

Five of the newcomers, he noticed, wore chaps and shirts gray with dust. As they came nearer the stubble on their hard, weather-pitted faces glistened with particles of alkali. It took but a glance to see they were ordinary cowhands. It was the sixth—a large man who flashed with silver from the crown of his ornate hat to the big-roweled spurs on his heels—who held Happy's attention. Rosettes and conchas decorated the fellow's chaps and bridle, both of which were of fine leather, stamped or burned with flowered figures. His saddle gleamed with silver mountings.

A smothered oath from Mournful set Happy's nerves on edge. Instantly he knew what had caused the exclamation. The pock-marked face of the newcomer was dark as that of any Indian. He wore a scraggly black mustache that drooped like tusks at the corners of his thick lips. The warning of the fortune-teller, Goldie Burton, flashed vividly to his mind. In spite of the manner in which he had ridiculed that warning, had laughed at Mournful's hunches, the appearance of the dark-complexioned fellow immediately following the stampede—which the *segundo* had predicted with such unerring accuracy, stirred a vague uneasiness within him.

The arrival of the strangers, who pulled rein before them, cut short his suddenly riotous thoughts.

"Howdy, jaspers," he greeted, his gray eyes sizing them up in a swift, critical glance. "Sure is hot, isn't it?"

"Howdy, yourself," the dark man returned in a heavy voice that rumbled in his throat like the thunder that now was becoming a constant grumble on the distant horizon. "Hadn't noticed the heat particular. But then, we're used to it. You must be from other parts. Where you bound?"

"Moving onto Powder River. To summer range," Happy crooked a careless leg around his saddle-horn, found his makin's and twisted a cigaret.

Yet for all his outward calm he was prey to a vague apprehension that increased momentarily under the newcomer's important air. The restless beady little eyes of the fellow's had shifted about, seemed to take in everything at a glance. Happy got but one good look at those eyes before they darted away to size up Mournful. When presently they traveled back to meet his steady gaze it seemed to him that an uneasy light had crept into them. He glanced at Mournful seeking the cause for it. The expression on the *segundo*'s face had not changed, unless perhaps it had become more doleful.

"What stuff you trailing?" the stranger demanded.

While the question was put to Happy, the nervous eyes were watching every move of Mournful, who had rolled himself a cigaret with deliberate slowness, fished a match from his pocket and lighted the quirly in cupped hands, lowered to keep the newcomer well within his range of vision.

"Rocking Chair!" For the first time in his life Happy found himself struggling to keep his tone civil. The flashing rosettes on the fellow's chaps, the flaming dust-covered shirt, thrown open at the neck, antagonized him. The sinister, beady eyes, the stolid, lantern-jawed face—everything about this stranger grated on Happy's taut nerves. Instinctively he was on his guard. Against what he did not know, unless, unconsciously, he had given credence to the warning of the girl fortune-teller at Halfway, and Mournful.

"Rocking Chair?" the stranger repeated, shooting a glance at his men that brought Happy's leg from around the horn to snap back into a sweaty stirrup. "Must be foreign stuff?"

"Dakota." Happy answered raspingly. "Ten hours off water . . . Damned nigh played out . . . How far do you figure the nearest water?"

Again the shifty eyes of the leader met those of his punchers in a quick, inscrutable glance.

"Powder River, fifteen mile or better west," the spokesman replied. "We just came from there. But it's high . . . Cut banks . . . Dangerous. Only one ford in twenty mile to water at. If it storms and the river's up you're plumb out of luck."

"Fifteen miles!" Happy ejaculated. "I thought it was a lot closer than that."

"Distances are deceiving in the badlands," the flashily garbed man remarked caustically.

"So I see." Happy gathered up his reins. "We'll have to make the best of it. Get going, you fellows!" he ordered his men, who paying no heed to the newcomers, had gone about getting the cattle to their feet and bunching them.

"Just a minute, mister—mister—" the dark man began sourly.

"Day!" Mournful put in quickly. "Happy Day!"

"Happy Day!" the big fellow repeated. In surprise Happy thought, daring another glance to place each one of his men. "I'm Al Keller, stock inspector. You don't suppose you happen to have any strays among that stuff a yours?"

Unable to tell from the fellow's words whether or not he knew of the stampeding herd, yet eager to have the thing over quickly so they could be on their way, it was on the tip of Happy's tongue to admit that there were strays among the Rocking Chairs. He caught Mournful's gaze. The *segundo*'s owlish eye winked warningly.

"Strays? Say, we haven't seen a stray this side of the line," Mournful lied before Happy could speak.

Dumfounded by the deliberate falsehood, Happy stared at him. But there was nothing on the solemn face to give him even an inkling of what was going on in the cowboy's mind.

"That being the case, of course you haven't any objection to my looking your herd over?" the man, Keller, suggested.

"None in the least, mister." It was Mournful who answered again, while with baleful gaze he watched the black clouds now tumbling up from the horizon. "Fact is, we'd like to have this herd of ours looked over. If you can find a stray in it we'll sure be plumb amazed."

Realizing from Keller's unfriendly attitude

the trouble in store for them as a result of the lie if the strays were found, Happy, cursing the *segundo* under his breath for his interference, cast about hastily for some plan to halt the inspection. But apparently Mournful, once started, was determined to carry out his bluff. If indeed, it was a bluff. Happy found himself doubting.

"Ride among them, jaspers. Look them over close," Happy now had no alternative but to urge. "They're plumb tuckered out. We've got to be moving quick onto water."

Waiting no further invitation, Keller motioned his men toward the cattle which, to Happy's disgust were scattering about to graze, thus giving the newcomers a far better opportunity of reading the brands than if they were bunched. As soon as the strange punchers were out of earshot, he whirled on Mournful angrily.

"You damned fool!" he exploded. "Have you gone plumb off your nut? Don't you see that jasper is hostile? His whole crew is snorting for trouble? What did you want to lie about those strays for? Suppose he finds them?"

"I was danged careful to be sure those strays were clean over to the other side of the herd before I spoke," Mournful replied. "With this storm coming up fast it won't be long till dark. I've got a hunch—"

"Lay off of those damned hunches for a while, will you?" Happy ground out. "They're all right when we want to laugh. . . . This is serious business. Even giving that walloper an opening to look the herd over will delay us. I was going to tell him we had them. . . . Make him go up the trail with us to get them if he was so damned anxious to."

"It isn't too late to do that yet if you're snorting for a row," Mournful stopped him maliciously.

"And get my foot into it with the law now?" Happy flung back. "You've made a fine mess of things. It looks like I'll have to go to lying to get us out of it—now."

"You can't tell that jasper anything he doesn't already know," Mournful observed, his eyes on the strangers, who were working through the herd with a speed and thoroughness that could only come from long experience with cattle. "It's up to us to bluff faster than he does."

"Do you think he's the one the herd got away from?" Happy asked.

Mournful pulled his gaze from the newcomers long enough to shoot Happy another of those inscrutable glances. "You're in Wyoming now," he remarked enigmatically. "A cow country where they play the game for big stakes. A thousand head of prime critters are worth a gamble any day in the week. . . . You've got to keep their nosey stock inspectors satisfied or they'll make life plumb hell for you. That's why I told him to go ahead and look the herd over."

“And probably got us into a pile of trouble doing it, too!” Happy grunted.

“You’d of been in a damned sight more trouble if you had of admitted the strays were there,” Mournful returned dryly. “Or if you had of tried to keep him from looking them over. I’ve got a hunch. I started this thing. I’m not all crazy. Let me finish it. If you’ll let me play it this once—alone—I’ll swear I’ll never mention another hunch to you as long as I live.” Happy would have sworn something of a twinkle flashed into the owlish eyes to vanish instantly. “You haven’t got any business with this walloper anyway,” Mournful was saying. “He’s a dark—”

He got no farther. Happy roweled away disgustedly. “All right,” he threw over his shoulder. “You lied us into it. Now get us out any way your crazy hunches figure. I won’t open my chops no matter how much you lie. But this herd is going to water, stock inspector or no stock inspector!”

Yet in spite of his announced determination to wash his hands of the whole affair, he chided himself bitterly for countenancing the *segundo*’s lie when he could not see the slightest reason for it. He resolved suddenly to tell Keller of the strays and thus offset any chance of being suspected of rustling. But, he reasoned quickly, Mournful had said he was playing another hunch. And, reluctantly, he was forced to the admission that Mournful’s hunches thus far had been amazingly correct. He was still pondering the thing when he rode up to Keller. “Seen anything?” he asked shortly.

“It’s getting too damned dark, with this storm coming up,” Keller grunted ill-naturedly. “But I’ll lay dough there are strays in this herd. . . . Just plenty of them.”

“Did you lose a bunch or something?”

Happy whirled at the casual inquiry to face Mournful, whom apparently he could not shake.

CHAPTER XII

"No," Keller snapped, his furtive gaze whipping between the two. "But there are heaps of others in this country who have. And when you say you haven't even sighted a stray somebody is—"

"I killed a jasper once for just such a remark as you are aiming to make," Mournful cut in with slow and deadly emphasis. "When I say we haven't seen a stray I mean we haven't seen a stray!"

Happy stared in utter amazement. Mournful's gaunt frame had suddenly lost its lazy sag; was rigidly taut, somehow gave him a flashing impression of spring steel, coiled, ready to unwind with a hiss. He sat for an instant gazing at this unknown *segundo.*

"There was a time when . . ." Mournful was rasping out through lips that were a thin grim line across tobacco-stained teeth. . . . "It took a damned good walloper to intimate I was lying . . ."

He lifted his horse with savage spurs, bolted over directly beside Keller, stuck a lean squared jaw into his face . . . "and it still does, jasper. Were you aiming to finish what you started to say?"

The moment was tense, filled with the possibility of gunplay. Clock-ticks passed; clock-ticks of suffocating heat that set beads of sweat to popping out on Keller's fat face. The thunder that rolled in rising crescendo seemed a part of the suddenly stark and deadly setting.

Happy held tight rein on violently straining muscles.

"We aren't to blame for what's been lost in these parts," he put in, roweling between the two, who sat motionless, glaring. "We haven't been across the line very long. . . . If this is a sample of the country I hope we don't have to stay. But we aren't going to fool around like this. Get that straight!"

"It's dead easy to tell you are from a country where they don't have trail laws," Keller found his voice to sneer. He licked dry lips. "But up here on Powder River we do things right. You're not moving this herd anywhere until I'm plumb satisfied there isn't a single stray in it." He spoke with the assurance of authority that momentarily impressed Happy.

"Why aren't you looking it over then, instead of sitting here chawing the rag?" Mournful demanded.

"I'm not in any particular rush," Keller threw back. "Besides, it will take a right smart of time. I'm going to work this herd!"

"Like hell you are!" Happy contradicted coldly. "Those critters are so tired they won't stand it.

Ride along with us if you want to, until we hit water. We'll bed down for the night and help you work it in the morning."

"I'm sorry, jasper," Keller said with obvious pleasure. "But I work a herd where I find it."

"I never heard of a stock inspector working a trail herd like this," Happy lashed out hotly. "Where I came from—"

"You've heard of it now, haven't you?" The smile Keller attempted was little more than a quirking of thick, weather-cracked lips. "We Wyoming stock inspectors have the right to work any herd, no matter where. . . . If we have reason to believe there are strays in it."

"And just what reason have you got to believe there are any strays in this herd?" Mournful inquired bitingly.

"Big bunches like this are bound to pick up strays," was Keller's quick reply. "If I don't spot them this side of Powder River I'm just out of luck. I don't mind telling you there are rustlers around here—just plenty of them—specially south of the rim. And we've got to be careful what crosses that river, for once they do they make the Pumpkin Butte country and we never see hide nor hair of them again."

"Were you a stock inspector in here last summer?" Mournful asked suddenly.

Keller shot him a swift, piercing glance. "No, I've just been on a few months. Why?"

"Nothing!" Mournful shrugged. "Only the Rocking Chair lost a thousand head in here somehow or another last spring. You stock inspectors are sure hell for leather when it comes to holding up and working half dead stuff, but it just strikes me that's all you're good for!"

"What do you mean?" Keller let go, his rage mounting.

"I didn't stutter any," the *segundo* returned, unperturbed. "But there isn't any use in us wasting any more time. We let you look this herd over; so you haven't got a holler of any kind coming there. You've been invited to come along and work it in the morning. You don't want to do that. . . . All right, jasper. We're pulling out right now. So-long!"

"Who in hell is boss of this outfit?" Keller demanded. "You or this young jasper?"

"Neither one of us," Mournful replied to the speechless amazement of Happy, who nevertheless let the lie pass without denial. "The boss rode up the trail hunting water just before you showed up. You must of seen him."

"I did see a jasper riding away at that," Keller admitted, crestfallen. "What's his name?"

"Jack Halliday!"

Happy stiffened perceptibly. He could have sworn that a look of relief crossed Keller's face. But he scarcely noticed it so occupied was he in pondering Mournful's new lie and attempting to find some reason for it. Jack Halliday, the dead foreman of the Rocking Chair! What had prompted Mournful to use that name? Why . . . Still he remained silent, watching the *segundo* closely. But as always, the mask-like expression offered not the slightest indication of what was going on in Mournful's mind.

"Who are you?" Keller demanded.

"Oh, just the *segundo*," wearily.

"Who is this jasper?" Keller indicated Happy.

"Told you once his name was Happy Day. He's just a cowhand."

"But he was giving orders round here?"

"I always keep him close when the boss is gone so I won't have to worry about the details," Mournful explained in a tiredly patient voice. "Now I reckon we'll be going. The boss said to follow him. . . . You know what orders are to cowhands. It's follow them or get your time. You wouldn't want us to lose our—"

"I'm working this herd right here and now!" Keller bawled. "Damn your boss. He isn't giving orders on Powder River. You aren't going to move a hoof!"

Dumfounded by the unfavorable turn events had taken, cursing Mournful under his breath for the lies that he was utterly at a loss to understand, Happy decided that things had reached a point where it was high time for him to intervene. Without so much as a glance at his *segundo*, he captured Keller's nervous gaze.

"You'll work this herd on water or you won't work it at all!" he said with cold determination.

"And what's more!" Mournful added, roweling up to where Happy could not fail to catch the furious winks of his owlish eyes, "you'll work it in broad daylight!"

"Just what are you intimating?" Keller roared, his swarthy wind-whipped skin the color of wet leather.

"Intimating?" Mournful took on an exaggerated air of hurt dignity. "What do you mean, intimating? I know the boss wouldn't stand for a bunch of strangers in the herd this late in the day. Why he'd go hell-crazy. We haven't got any proof of who you really are."

"I'll show you who I am!" Keller thundered. He jerked back an ornate vest to reveal a badge pinned on a livid shirt. "That's who I am. A stock inspector! And I'm going to work this herd—here and now!"

Mournful turned pained eyes on Happy. "Just head them up the trail, jasper!" he ordered in a voice deadly in its calm. "Stock inspectors haven't got authority to let a thousand head of thirsty cows suffer while they're working them for strays—even in Wyoming."

Satisfied by now that Mournful had some motive for his strange actions—and possibly also a plan to get them safely through the crisis, which at the moment seemed well nigh hopeless without gunplay—Happy held his tongue and started toward the herd.

"Hold on!" Keller bawled, roweling after him. "You move those critters and I'll arrest you for—"

"For what?" Mournful's mount snorted a protest as he lifted it with savage rowels and sat it on its haunches beside them. His owlish eyes had narrowed to slits, glinted dangerously. "For what, jasper?"

"For—for . . ." The stock inspector licked his fat lips. His nervous gaze whipped about like that of a trapped beast. "For—for not obeying the range laws of Wyoming," he blurted out lamely.

"But we've invited the law to ride with us. . . . Offered to spend all the time needed to work the herd in daylight after these critters get on water," Happy pointed out coldly. "What more can we do?"

"Hold them right here like I ordered you to!" Keller roared.

"And let a walloper who claims to be a stock inspector; a walloper we don't know from Adam's off ox, get them all riled up after dark and mebbeso stampede them from here to hell and gone?" Mournful shot in. "Not on your life, jasper. Anybody can buy a badge and make a flash with it." He jerked a gnarled thumb toward Happy. "Trail them out, kid!"

Completely bewildered now by Mournful's

deliberate and continued interruptions, yet realizing that the *segundo*'s play left nothing to do but carry on the bluff, Happy again started away. A curse brought him about. Keller had whipped out his forty-five, sat his mount rigid, the Colt plastered against his hip. "Move a head of these critters and you're under arrest for rustling!" the inspector bellowed. "I know damned well there are strays in that herd."

"If you're so dead sure of it you'd be willing to come along with us!" Mournful flung back. "Far as that thing goes . . ." He eyed the Colt with cold contempt. ". . . We aren't half as scared of it as you are to use it. . . . Because we're not defying the law . . . We've got sense enough to know you'll get your foot into it up to your neck if you cut loose. But if you really have got a hankering to, don't hold back on our account. We'll show you how quick our gun-slinging waddies will make duck soup of your whole gang. You aren't monkeying with natives, now, feller. You're twisting tails with jaspers who will eat you up guts, feathers and all. We let you look over this herd, willingly; you didn't find anything. Now we're through rag-chewing. Our boss told us to make water by dark. You're plumb welcome to come along. But don't try to stop us, 'cause we aren't going to be stopped; even if we have to tromp down all the stock inspectors this side of hell!"

It was a long and laborious speech for the solemn-faced Mournful. But his voice grew quieter and more deadly with every word. Yet no one had difficulty in hearing him. Before he had finished Keller was shifting uneasily in his saddle, his face black with apoplectic fury.

"Just try moving a single critter," the stock inspector snarled, reining back to join his men, who had ridden up one by one, beside him. "Just try it if you feel lucky!"

CHAPTER XIII

Sensing trouble, the Rocking Chair punchers too galloped up, jerked rein, went taut in their saddles, thumbs hooked in the cartridge belts that sagged at their waists. Happy sat his mount motionless as a statue, the knuckles of his hands white with pressure from gripping the horn. The sun, a blazing ball, hung for a time above the fast-traveling, inky clouds, then sank from sight to shoot golden shafts high into the heavens. A vast silence, like that found in chambers of the dead, lay over the badlands. The air itself became inert and stifling. No one seemed to be aware of it but Keller. Again great beads of sweat popped out on his forehead. He swiped them away nervously with the back of his gun hand.

Then, of a sudden, a breeze, cooled by distant rain, whined across the sickening flats. A big steer threw up its head, sniffed water and bawled pleadingly. The bellow echoed along the line in a thousand different tones, rose into a deafening tumult. Instantly the herd was in motion, headed up the trail in the direction from which the scent of water had come.

"Stop them! Stop them!" Keller thundered coming to life, and standing in one stirrup. "I give you fair warning!"

"Stop them, hell!" Mournful threw back savagely. "We can't stop these thirsty critters now that they've got a smell of water. Even a stock inspector in Wyoming can't do that. We'll be lucky if they don't stampede. God help you if there are any lost. I know one jasper claiming to be a stock inspector who'll have just plenty to answer for in court."

"You will stop them!" Keller yelled. "Here, jasper, you aren't going to give me the slip under cover of dark like that. Come back here!" he threw after Happy, who had whirled his horse and started away for the point.

"And lose a thousand head of stuff?" Happy flashed. "Not by a damned sight. These critters—"

Keller's forty-five laced the lowering gloom with flame. Happy's horse sagged, went to its knees, tried valiantly to right itself, then crumpled beneath him. Quick as the thing happened, Happy barely had time to throw himself clear of the brute as it hit the ground to beat its head savagely and kick up a curtain of dust.

In an instant he was on his feet. But strangely for Happy, he made no move to draw. The cattle were pouring over the rim into the ravine. The Rocking Chair punchers hesitated, torn between the duty of attempting to stem the mad rush and loyalty to Happy. Keller sat his horse, the smoke from his hot-barreled Colt wreathing about his head in the dead calm air.

"You jaspers catch that herd!" It was Mournful who shot the cool order at the cowboys.

Still the men hung back, waiting for Happy to speak. "Just say the word," one of them pleaded of him. "We'll show these badland rats where to get off at. Just say it. . . . One . . ."

"Don't one of you dare drag an iron!" Happy snapped out. "Follow those critters like the devil himself was after you. Stick to them. . . . Heel fly them . . . Till hell freezes over."

The punchers quit him reluctantly, galloped away to overtake the bawling herd, which was crossing the ravine at a lumbering trot.

In a half dozen swift bounds Happy was beside Keller, whose gaze again was whipping back and forth between him and Mournful, obviously suspicious of the *segundo*'s claim that the boss had ridden up the trail.

"You killed my horse, you big pot-bellied—!" Happy said in a tone that rang like chilled steel. "It's a poor swap. A damned poor swap. . . . But I'm forking your nag. . . . See what the law says about that. Climb down. . . . Climb down, jasper or I'll drag you . . ."

"I had a right to shoot!" Keller bellowed, making a threatening gesture with his forty-five. "And I'll kill you too. . . . If you get hostile. You were resisting the law!"

"Like hell I was!" Happy retorted. "I didn't start that herd. And there isn't any law on earth that can stop them now they've got a whiff of water. Get off that nag, jasper!"

"You—!" Keller snarled. "I'll—"

Quick as a flash Happy shoved his arm beneath the fellow's leg and the stirrup guard. With a mighty wrench he dragged him from the saddle to pitch headlong and go sprawling in the dust. The Colt flew from his fingers as he hurtled through the air. Yet with surprising agility for a man of such ponderous bulk he leaped to his feet.

"Kill him! Kill him!" he bellowed to his men. "Kill the rustler. He's trying to give us the slip. Unlimber, you—"

Happy dared a glance over his shoulder. Keller's men had gone for their guns. But they came away from their holsters only to be tossed to the ground. Mournful, his face a study of ludicrous sadness, hunched in his saddle, his own forty-five menacing the crew.

"That's right, throw them down, jaspers!" he was whining. "Talk about you killing anybody, you warble-backed, white-livered . . . I've got just enough ca'tridges in this Colt of mine here to pump you all down and still have one left for the next rattler I run across."

At that moment Keller rushed Happy, head down, bawling like an infuriated bull. Waiting until the fellow was almost upon him, Happy side-stepped neatly and sent him lurching back with a short-arm blow that connected with his chin.

"I'll kill you, you—!" Keller bawled. Dazed though he was by the blow, his rage became a frenzy. "I'll kill you. . . . You . . ." He came back blindly. "You're under arrest for resisting an officer. What the hell's holding you jaspers?" he rasped over his shoulder at his staring men. "Why don't you crack down on him?"

"Your men won't crack down on anybody or anything as long as old Rocking Chair Davis is holding the pat hand," Mournful taunted as Happy jabbed the stock inspector three times in the face before he could cover up.

"I don't need them," Keller bawled crazily. "Don't need any kind of help. I'll take this walloper into camp alone. . . . Choke the life out of him once I get my hands on you!" Shaking his head savagely, he bored in, trying to grapple with Happy, who to all appearances would have stood little show once the great arms closed about him. But his great weight, the blasting heat that set sweat to trickling down across his pouchy face, put Keller at a disadvantage. Happy side-stepped to smash him behind the ear as he floundered past. Keller wheeled. Happy danced around him, landing rapid-fire blows that opened the swarthy skin across his cheek, closed one eye and finally brought the blood gushing from his nose.

"Give up or I'll kill you!" Keller panted.

"Give up or you'll kill me?" Happy jerked out. "Giving up to a pot-bellied stray like you isn't my style even if you were making any show of taking me." He set himself, feinted with his left and shot a sizzling right to the point of Keller's jaw. It stopped the bellowing inspector. He rocked on his heels, lurched backwards. His eyes went glassy. His knees began to buckle. Quick to follow up his advantage, Happy bounded forward, lifted another blow from the ground. It landed with a smack over Keller's heart. The inspector went sprawling on his back in the dirt.

Happy spun about. His hand flashed down. Quick as a striking snake his Colt was from his holster, clutched at his hip to sweep Keller's dumfounded crew.

"I'm all set for them now, Mournful!" he panted. "You take the herd. They'll travel till they hit water. But be damned careful they don't get away from you." He dared an anxious glance at the sky. By now ragged-edged clouds were rolling and twisting over the buttes, drab and austere in the mantle of evening, ugly, sinister in the deepening gloom of the approaching storm. "Try and make Powder River ahead of this storm. Push them across if you can. I'm depending on you!"

Mournful nodded solemnly, holstered his Colt and stared down at the flashily-garbed Keller, prone on the ground. "Is he dead?" he inquired with mock anxiety.

"You can't kill a barrel-headed walloper like him by just hitting him with your fist," Happy snorted.

"You sure trimmed him proper!" Mournful observed admiringly. "But don't you think you'd better finish him off?"

"Finish him off?" Happy blurted out. "You don't mean . . . Say, I'd rather plug myself than to kill a jasper who is down and can't . . . What's eating on you? You're talking like you're out of your head."

"He'll just get you later for the whipping you gave him if you don't." Mournful shrugged resignedly. "I've got a hunch—"

"Let up on those hunches!" Happy yelled. "Catch the critters. They're traveling like the mill-tails of hell!"

"All right! All right!" Mournful agreed testily, but still making no move to leave. He turned a leisurely eye on the angry sky, aglow with sheet lightning. "I'm plumb willing to go after those critters. . . . But . . .You might need help. They're still five to one!"

"Don't waste any more time chewing the rag," Happy flashed. "Cross the river ahead of flood water if you can. I'll find you. If I don't right off, I'll meet you somewhere south." He sidled over to Mournful, who leaned from his saddle, without taking his gaze from the motionless crew. "Come daylight, cut those strays from the herd and turn them back. If Keller ever finds them now our goose is cooked proper."

"Keller will never find them in our herd," Mournful said coolly. "So-long!" Without offering any explanation he roweled away into the deepening gloom, leaving Happy, speechless with surprise, wondering what he had meant.

When he had disappeared in the lowering light up the trail Happy maneuvered to a position where he could watch the crew and still keep one eye on the motionless Keller. Then he backed to Keller's horse and eased himself into the silver-mounted saddle, his Colt ever holding the punchers at bay. At that moment the inspector stirred, blinked, struggled to his elbow.

"Get off of that horse!" he gasped out. "You're under arrest, I tell you. I'll show you who is boss in this country. Where did the critters go. Damn you!"

"Yonder!" Happy jerked a thumb up the trail in the direction in which the herd already had been swallowed up in the falling darkness. "They'll be on water before long. We'll either cross Powder River or hold them on this side—all depends on this storm. If there are any strays we'll cut them back come daylight. See you in the morning. So-long!"

Reining Keller's horse about, he roweled into

the ravine. Instantly the five leaped to the ground, seized up their guns and remounted.

"Catch that jasper!" Keller thundered, lurching to his feet and securing the forty-five he had dropped when Happy jerked him from the saddle. "He'll give us the slip sure as hell tonight." The five spurred away in pursuit. "Here, hold on a minute! Can't you see I'm afoot? One of your nags will have to pack double. Damn that walloper! He'll pay dear for stealing my horse and saddle!"

Disgustedly the five jerked rein and rode back. One of the crew swung down sullenly, turned his mount over to the fuming inspector and vaulted up behind the saddle of a companion. Keller climbed aboard stiffly.

"Now catch him!" he roared. "Catch that jasper first if you have to kill him. Then the herd!" Again the crew started after Happy. But as before they came to a sudden halt on the edge of the ravine.

"Not so fast, fellows," came the cool voice of the youth, from just under the rim. "This here trail isn't healthy tonight. . . . It won't be until our critters get water. You'd better wait till daylight."

"I'll bring a posse down here in the morning and blow the whole bunch of you to hell!" Keller bawled furiously.

"Suit yourself about that!" Happy flung back.

"But you'll do it tomorrow instead of tonight. I said you were back-trailing. . . ."

There was no mistaking the determination in the voice. And having seen him in action, in spite of their numbers, the men had no stomach for risking an encounter with him. Unmindful of the fuming Keller's orders, they turned and started down the trail at a gallop. With no alternative, the inspector, a ludicrous figure in the gloom, one eye swollen and discolored, his face smeared with blood and sweat, his silver trappings dulled and grimy with dirt, took in after them, cursing at the top of his voice.

It was not until they had been lost in the gloom that Happy remounted Keller's horse and started along the trail after the Rocking Chair herd. The swift movements of the animal seemed to ease the tumult of his thoughts. The whole affair, which on the surface had seemed so natural, suddenly appeared as a mystery, made more baffling by Mournful's uncanny hunches and strange actions.

Why had Mournful taken it upon himself to lie about the strays in the herd when the truth would have sufficed and certainly could have caused no more trouble? Why had he lied about the boss of the herd being absent? Why had he called him Jack Halliday?

The more he pondered the maze of questions the more incomprehensible they became. Of only one thing was he sure. That was that he was going to call Mournful to account at the first opportunity, demand an explanation and warn him hereafter to play his hunches when they in nowise interfered with the progress of the trail herd.

A vivid flash of lightning that tore the sky from zenith to horizon, followed by a deafening clap of thunder that seemed to rock the badlands, startled him from his retrospection. His glance flew to the heavens. They were entirely overcast by black clouds now, streaked with green, that rolled and twisted angrily.

"It would be a hell of a note to lose that herd in a stampede after what we just got them through," he mused aloud. "If I can catch them before the storm breaks, or before that damned Mournful has another hunch, mebbyso I can do something." He strained ahead for a glimpse of the cattle. He could see nothing in the darkness, nor could he hear any sound save the crash and reverberations of thunder.

He lifted his horse with the rowels. It shot ahead in a gravel-flinging lunge.

CHAPTER XIV

A short distance and thickening gloom forced Happy to slacken his pace to a running walk. The farther he rode the more difficult it became to follow the trail, which presently was blotted out altogether. He roweled along, pulling up from time to time to listen. But the Rocking Chair herd might well have vanished from the region for all he was able to see or hear of it above the swiftly-approaching storm.

"That's damned queer, unless the scent of water or the thunder already has started them to running like a bunch of scared jacks," he muttered after an infinity of time consumed in hopeless search. "It's a cinch if this horse of Keller's has got a lick of sense he's still following the trail." To convince himself, however, he dismounted. Squaring around until his back was to the steadily-rising wind, he struck a match, shielded it in his cupped hands. The horse, snorting and lunging back on the reins, extinguished the tiny light. But by its single, timid flare he could see nothing of the trail. He wasted several minutes crawling around on all fours hunting for tracks. Finally he abandoned the search, straightened up thoroughly bewildered. Convinced however, that his sense of direction—inherent in every rider of the range—had not deserted him even in the darkness, he remounted and rode on.

"This nag I took from Keller has quit that trail to head for home!" he snorted disgustedly after a time. "It'd be a fine mess if it packed me into that inspector's hang-out." He strained anxiously through the now ebon void ahead. "Damn it all, I wish I could locate the herd." He spoke aloud after the manner of men of the silent trails who make confidants of their mounts on long weary miles. "I'm liable to be needed bad in camp. Cuss that hunch-playing Mournful anyhow. If it hadn't been for him I'd still be with the critters. Those hunches of his are all bum steers. But . . ." He jerked the reins as the pony stumbled and went down to bump along dangerously on its knees before it finally regained its balance and jerked straight. ". . . somehow they seem to come true. Just because this Keller happened to be a dark-complected gent I don't suppose I'll ever hear the last of what that Goldie Burton warned me. . . . Pick up your feet you damned crow-bait," as the horse stumbled again. "If you haven't got sense enough to follow a trail at least you ought to be able to keep from busting your own fool neck. I wish the Old Man had kept Mournful at the Rocking Chair." When the horse had steadied down. "I like him; but I never worried in my life until he got to springing those fool hunches. He's worked on me now until I'm almost beginning to believe them myself." A vivid streak of lightning that shivered across the sky to leave a blinding glare before his eyes long after it had faded, pulled him violently from his thoughts. The boom of thunder that followed brought the horse to a dead stop, trembling with fear.

Then it began to rain. At first large pelting drops borne in on a wind that suddenly arose to a sinister hiss. Happy lifted his hat to let it splatter on his head.

"If Mournful didn't get to the river this rain will do those critters a world of good," he mused. "That is, providing they didn't get scared and run like all hell was after them. I wish I knew where they were."

Suddenly the storm broke with fury. Rain was loosed in torrents; whipped by the screaming wind, it struck him full in the face, brought the horse about, rump to the cutting drops. Jerking down his hat and ducking his head, he hunched up in his saddle and roweled ahead again.

In a few seconds the storm had become a deluge. Lightning ripped the sky in blinding flashes, revealing buttes that loomed like somber, eerie monsters behind gray sheets of wind-driven rain. Thunder crashed and rolled with each new hissing livid bolt; reverberated endlessly through the badlands.

Presently the pony came to a dead stop. The lacing rowels only brought forth sullen grunts.

But the brute refused to budge in its tracks. With the knowledge of a man of the range, who early learns to rely on the instinct of his horse, Happy quickly abandoned his efforts to force it on. Somewhere ahead in the inky blackness he knew the brute had sensed danger. Dismounting, he held on to the bridle reins, and started edging forward cautiously. A flare of lightning momentarily lighted the region. He leaped back. He stood perilously near the brink of a yawning cañon. He hunched with his back to the storm, waiting for the next flash. When it came, he peered down. Far below, a tumbling mass of yellow, foam-crested water, churned Powder River.

"Good old horse," he said, stroking the pony's flaring nose while he tried to pierce the stygian gloom. "A few more steps and you and me would have taken our last dive. You're a hell of a horse," he growled in the next breath. "Quit the trail and lead me way off here forty mile from nowhere. Haven't you got a home—some place you were aiming to get to? You—"

He broke off abruptly, stood breathless listening to another sound he had caught above the boom of the storm. It was a distant roar, increasing so rapidly in volume that soon it was battering on his eardrums.

"Hail!" he muttered. "We've got to find cover!" Careful to turn the brute away from the cañon, he found his stirrup, swung up and gave it the rowels. But the terrified horse only hung back trembling.

Louder, louder grew the roar until it was deafening. Knowing through experience the savage, merciless battering, sometimes death that lay behind that sinister roar, he leaped down, uncinched and dragged off the saddle. Slipping the bridle over the ears of the pony, he gave it a slap. With a wild snort of relief it bolted away into the lightning-riddled darkness.

"Good luck, old fellow," he shouted after it.

Before he could squat on his heels and pull the heavy saddle over his head for protection the hail was upon him. First tiny pellets that bounced away gaily, streaks of white visible even in the blackness. Then a terrific crash as the pellets became great balls of ice that dented the saddle and battered it down upon his head. The roar now was thunderous, rising in a crescendo volume. The hail piled up like drifts of snow about him. The cold crept to the marrow of his bones. His soaked clothing clung to his shivering form.

Then to add to the horror of the moment came a mighty boom. No need for a rangeman to ask its cause. Powder River on a rampage was gnawing at its banks. A great section had given way. It sent him crowding back, hanging grimly to the saddle on his head. On and on he crawled, one dripping, freezing hand clutching the saddle skirt, the other groping blindly in the ice-cold ooze. He went forward blindly, his back and hips bruised by the hail, his only hope that he could find some shelter from the merciless assault.

"Keller's foxy saddle is going to be in nice shape," was the ludicrous thought he gave voice to as he paused for breath. "I don't suppose that will make any hit with him either; but I'm danged lucky I got it. God, but that hail is coming down! The worst I ever saw. Guess Ed Jackson wasn't so crazy after all when he told about the storms up here. Sure would beat the brains out of a man in no time . . . Wish I knew where the herd is . . . And Mournful and the boys . . . I hope the critters will stand." Sudden fear for the safety of his Rocking Chair crew, for the moment overshadowed his own predicament. "Aw, hell," he muttered, "Mournful has held more herds in storms than I ever have. I'll bet that hunch-playing, lying old lobo has got them sheltered somewhere and the boys are all right."

A sudden slackening of the icy pellets gave hope that the hail, like most prairie hailstorms, would pass as quickly as it started. But to his surprise the roar increased, after the slight let up, became even louder. Hail seemed to drop in sheets from the inky heavens to send him crawling along again.

He had gone but a short distance when, without warning, his feet slipped from under him. He clutched wildly for the saddle; missed it. Before he could regain his balance he felt himself falling. Down, down, into the darkness, clawing madly for something to cling to, the hail beating him mercilessly on his now unprotected head and shoulders.

He struck ground with a jolt that knocked the breath from his body. Half dazed though he was from the tumble, he realized what had happened. He had crawled over the brink of one of the deep ravines that gashed the badlands.

For a second he lay stunned and panting. Then the slicing pain of the icy balls drove him to action. He struggled to his feet, shielding his head with his hands, choking back the groans as the hail slashed at him cruelly. Abandoning hope of finding the saddle, which he knew was somewhere on the rim above, he groped about blindly for the bank to huddle against. Before he could locate it the downpour forced him to squat and burrow his head beneath his arms. But not for long could he endure this battering. Pains stabbed his body, which was growing numb from the hailstones beating down upon him.

Knowing that his one hope lay in locating the bank, which would afford some protection until he could gouge out a hole with his spur rowels, he climbed up and sloshed about in the darkness. His sense of direction had deserted him. Gritting his teeth on the stinging pain, he plunged on gamely. Time and again he went down to sprawl full-length in the mud. The breath tore at his lungs. He felt nauseated, dizzy from the grueling punishment inflicted by the hail. Keeping his head covered as best he could, he staggered in all directions. But apparently the ravine was of considerable width and he had wandered into the center, for he could find neither bank.

He knew he could not hold out much longer. Fatigue finally sent him to his knees. He doubled up, let the hailstones beat against him, only vaguely conscious of the pain they inflicted as they battered him then went bouncing away into the darkness.

He got up again, tried to stagger on. A few paces and he went down. A blow from a hailstone on the temple set his brain to reeling. His faculties seemed to have halted. His body had become pulp, devoid of feeling. He was dully aware that he was on the ground, writhing and groaning. The sluicing roar of his own hot blood in his ears now drowned out that of the hail. A ball of ice struck him a stunning blow on the head. He lurched to his feet, pitched forward. His outstretched hands encountered the bank. His last conscious thought was of dragging himself against it.

How long he lay Happy never knew. When he regained his senses he cowered back, expecting another blow on the head. When it did not come he stared about groggily. The roar had ceased.

A vast silence shrouded the badlands. Far down the ravine he could see the buttes standing out in sharp silhouette against a full moon which drenched the hail-mantled region with a silver sheen. He raised stiffly on one elbow. He was hugging the gumbo bank of the ravine. About him were small drifts of hailstones. His body was still numb from the battering and the intense cold. Gritting his teeth on the pain, he climbed to his feet and braced himself against the bank until his head stopped spinning.

When he had succeeded in getting some control over himself, he started limping across the ravine. As the warm blood began circulating he felt better, although the bruises on his head and shoulders throbbed painfully.

Reaching the opposite bank presently, he climbed up onto the greasewood flat and looked about. Far ahead and to his left he sighted a tiny light. Fearful that it was a star he watched it until his eyes filled with tears. But it did not move nor vanish. Taking heart, he started toward it, forcing his weary body along painfully, stopping from time to time to sink in his tracks and rest before he could summon strength to proceed.

After a seemingly endless period the light loomed large before him—a penciled ray emanating from a window. He staggered toward it, but now that refuge was so close at hand it seemed he could not hold out to reach it. All the punishment he had endured centered in one horrible moment and came crashing down upon him. He made a valiant effort to go on. His legs suddenly had grown wooden with weariness and cold. The throbbing in his battered head blurred his vision. The warm blood coursing through the bruises on his back seared like livid welts. He stumbled and fell. Several seconds passed before he could summon the strength to rise.

On the point of collapse, he staggered against the side of a house and groped along until he reached a door. Bracing himself against the jamb, he found the knob, kicked open the door and reeled inside. With an oath a man seated beside a table upset his chair and came lurching to his feet. Blinded for an instant by the light, Happy brushed his eyes with the back of his hand. When he was able to see he started violently. The man was Al Keller, one eye swollen shut, his cheeks badly bruised and discolored. And behind him was a woman; a woman with a strangely familiar face.

Happy got but a fleeting glance at her. Another oath left Keller's lips. He grabbed for his Colt. The woman screamed. A jet of flame laced across the room. A slicing pain ripped through Happy's forearm. The ceaseless echoes of the report of the forty-five crashed down upon him. He put what remaining strength he had into an effort to leap back. But instead he felt himself impelled forward by some irresistible force. He tried to stop. But mind and body refused to coordinate. He threw out his arms, pitched face downward to the floor!

CHAPTER XV

Clock-ticks passed. How many Happy never knew. Stunned but still conscious, he lay on the floor of the cabin like dead, eyes tightly closed. To move, he knew, would draw the fire of Keller, who he could hear above him. There was an endless, nerve-racking moment of silence, broken only by hoarse breathing. Then Happy caught the sound of running feet outside. Came Keller's voice, apparently turning back a group of excited punchers at the door with the explanation that he needed no help and that no one had been hurt. The tension snapped. The girl screamed. Again the terror in that scream cleared Happy's brain. With a maudlin laugh Keller slammed and bolted the door. The footsteps of the retreating men died away.

"You'll pay for this!" The girl's cry beat on Happy's mind, which suddenly had become alert. "If you've killed him . . ." Fury choked her.

That voice! In vain Happy searched his memory trying to recall where he had heard that voice which now struck him as vaguely familiar as her face. But he had little time to think. She was crossing the room, had dropped to her knees beside him, and was trying frantically to lift him.

"Put up that gun, Keller!" she blazed fearlessly.

"You've gone as far as you dare. You'll regret tonight's work to your dying day!"

Spur rowels jangled noisily. Happy knew Keller had shifted nervously.

"The devil I will!" came Keller's voice sneeringly. "If that lousy jasper is dead it serves him right. He hadn't any business tying up with me in the first place. He's the walloper who smashed me in the eye—when I wasn't looking. He stole my horse and saddle. I'll—"

"You'll help me move him to a bed, that's what you'll do," she cried, still tugging at Happy, who hung limp to keep her from turning him over. "And you'll do everything you can to save him, you coward! Couldn't you see he was exhausted; had been out in that terrible hailstorm? Don't you ever give anyone a fighting chance? Help me lift him, I say!"

Keller laughed; a great, booming laugh that yet carried a sinister note. But apparently the stinging scorn in her voice roused him to action, for by the sounds above Happy knew that the stock inspector was holstering his .45. Came a heavy step, a long-drawn sigh. The big fellow strode over to him, stooped, seized him roughly under the arm pits and started dragging him across the floor.

Bundling his logy muscles for one mighty effort, Happy wrenched himself loose and bounded to his feet. His fist found Keller's face in a crunching blow. Happy turned ashen with the effort. But summoning his strength, before the inspector could collect his wits and go for his gun Happy swung again. This time his fist landed at the base of Keller's ear. The big fellow grunted, went reeling backwards, dropped like a log.

Happy spun about. So quickly had the thing happened that the girl with the strangely familiar face was still on her knees, staring up at him through terror-stricken eyes. Reeling over to her, he helped her to her feet.

"You—aren't—hurt—badly?" she gasped in fright.

"He just creased my forearm," Happy said grimly. "I'm sorry to raise a rumpus in front of you, though . . . I wouldn't of come but I was all in. . . . I had to get somewhere. I didn't know Keller was here." The room began to whirl about him. He felt his knees buckling. He reached out wildly for support. His fingers closed on thin air. Then he was going down again.

When his brain had cleared he stared around hazily. He was stretched full-length on the floor. Added to the other horrible aches of his body was a sharp pain in his forearm that sickened him. He raised it weakly. It had been bandaged.

"Do you feel better now?" asked a cool, sweet voice.

Things came rushing back to him with startling vividness. "Hell, yes!" he blurted out, getting to his feet to back against the wall, panting, and face the girl. "Did Keller . . ."

"Take it easy," she cautioned, advancing and forcing him gently into a chair. "Here, drink this!" She pressed a steaming toddy to his lips. "I found a bottle in Keller's pocket. He's . . . ." She glanced fearfully toward a corner. ". . . He's been drinking." Happy followed her gaze. On the floor, bound and gagged, was the stock inspector, his discolored face purple with anger and the exhaustion of clawing at his fetters.

"Honest to . . ." Happy blurted out blankly. "A little bit of a thing like you didn't hog-tie that big walloper, did you?"

"Yes," she answered. "He was powerless."

"Are . . . are you his wife?" he asked almost timidly.

"No!" tartly.

"Sister?"

"No relation at all, thank goodness!"

"What outfit is this?" His blood-shot eyes swept the room which was like all other ranch-house dining rooms he had seen; bare log walls, rafters dingy with smoke and age—a single, dirty window in the rear wall through which he had sighted moonlight—a rusty heating stove on top of which simmered a pan of water—a few sturdy cane-bottomed chairs, and an oil-cloth-covered table, on which burned a kerosene lamp with a smutty globe.

"The 'Circle H' on Powder River," she said.

His survey of the room complete, he fingered his throbbing arm gingerly, suddenly self-conscious and embarrassed before her. "Say," he gulped, scuffing the floor with the toe of his boot, "your face is familiar. I've seen you before." He gave her a timid, sidelong glance. "You're—you're—" He stopped, blankly, cudgeled his logy brain for an answer.

"I knew you when you came in," she encouraged shyly. "You're Happy Day!"

"And you . . ." He summoned courage to look at her closely. "You're . . . You're . . ."

Came to him in a flash the fair at Halfway. An exceptionally pretty golden-haired, blue-eyed girl warning him of a dark man coming into his life.

"You're Goldie Burton, the fortune-teller from the fair at Halfway!" he said excitedly. "But where did you come from? What are you doing way up here on Powder River?"

"You did remember, didn't you?" she smiled—a winning smile, pretty arched lips across pearly teeth. But there was nervousness in the smile, he thought. "I'll have to put off answering questions until later," she was saying. "You've got to get rested quickly. Then—"

"Then what?" he tore his gaze from her to ask. "Is that dark man you warned me about coming to raise a ruckus?"

Warmed by the toddy and temporarily forgetful of his aches and pains in the tumult of thoughts which poured into his mind, Happy was beginning to get a grip on himself. Now that his first flush of embarrassment had passed, he gazed at her admiringly. While he never had admitted it, he had been just a little jealous of Mournful.

"I don't know," her soft husky voice interrupted his musing. "But something is going to happen. After your trouble with Keller it won't be well for you to be found here. I'm sorry you wandered into the Circle H. . . . But as long as you did we must make the best of it; and get away again as quickly as we can."

"Get away?" he asked in surprise. "I don't want to get away."

"But we must," she cried.

He stared at her puzzled. "Mebbyso," he admitted, thrilled, but uncomprehending the "we" she had used. "What is there for me to run from? If we did go, where do you figure on heading this time of night?"

"Anywhere!" There was desperation, a pleading note in her voice.

"What did you come here for if you want to get away so bad?" The moment he gave it utterance he was sorry for the question.

"I didn't."

"You're here, aren't you?"

"Yes. . . . But Keller . . ."

"Keller what?" as she hesitated.

"Keller brought me here. . . ." There was a frantic note of appeal in her voice. "He and his men caught me alone on the trail after dark. They made me come."

"Then you're a prisoner?" he demanded, suspiciously in spite of himself. "What for?"

"Oh, I can't tell you about it now. We haven't time—they're liable to come any minute."

"Who is liable to come any minute?" His persistent stubbornness amazed him. "I don't know what you're talking about."

"I guess I don't either," she admitted with a childishly hopeless gesture. "But please hurry." She broke off to cross to the door and listen. "They'll be coming in a minute!" She ran back to him, stood before him, her eyes wide with some unknown fear, beseeching.

"Who'll be coming?" he asked blankly. "That dark man you—"

"Keller's men." Her interruption was nervous, almost terrified. "All but four of them rode away directly after the storm to meet somebody—I don't know who." Again she listened fearfully. "Please hurry!"

"What of it?" he demanded carelessly. "What if they all come in here? I feel a heap better since I got thawed out a little. I haven't done anything to run from anybody. Don't worry, Miss. I'll danged soon find out what the rip is—them holding you prisoner."

"No! No!" she cried hastily. "Let's escape while we have the chance."

The eyes she turned on him were frank and pleading. In spite of himself Happy's gaze fell.

"Sounds queer to me," he managed to get out. "But I'm getting used to queer things up here in the badlands. Who owns this Circle H spread? Keller?"

"I don't know. I'm trying to find out. When I do . . . But please . . . We haven't time now." She sped back to the door to listen again. "I was going to escape alone. But I knew I couldn't make it in the storm. Don't you feel strong enough to go with me now?"

"I feel all right." He got to his feet gingerly to stand for a moment half expecting the room to start pitching. But apparently his brain was clear for he was steady. Save for a dull throbbing of the bruises made by the hail-stones, and the pain in his forearm, he felt almost like his old self. "But I'm not going to light out of here when I don't even know where I'm going or what for. . . . I've got to locate my herd as quick as it gets daylight."

"Then you're a coward like all the rest of them," she flared, her lips curling with scorn. "You're not afraid I'll hurt you, are you? I need help desperately!"

"I have never been called a coward." Happy winced under her scorn. His cool retort was a bluff. "But if streaking off in the night without even knowing where a jasper is headed, or what for, is being a coward I reckon I am one."

"I thought perhaps you would trust me!" she pleaded. "You're a man. . . . Can fight with men . . . I'm a woman. . . . I can't. . . . But if we don't get away . . ."

"I'll go!" Happy hung his head sheepishly, shamed by the scorn in her tone. "Which way?"

Seizing hold of his uninjured arm, she pulled him eagerly to the window. She tugged at it with all her strength. The weather had swollen the frame, sealed it fast.

"I can't budge it!" she whispered desperately.

She spun about to look for some other way out aside from the door by which he had entered. Her eyes rested for an instant on Keller. Her gaze grew wild, startled. In the fellow's struggles to free himself the improvised gag had been dislodged from his mouth. He let forth a lusty bawl for help.

Completely baffled by the girl's secretiveness and strange actions which, it seemed, were actuated as much by a fear for his safety as for her own, and strongly determined now to humor her until such time as it was light enough to pick up the trail of his herd, Happy jerked out his .45, shattered the pane with the butt. Knocking off the ragged edges of glass, he helped the girl through. At that moment the punchers came running from the bunkhouse in answer to Keller's cries. Leaping to the table, Happy blew out the light. Bounding through the window, he joined the girl.

"Make the big ravine!" she said in a low voice. "It's only a few hundred yards."

"We've got to get horses," he said, hanging back. "A cowhand can't run anywhere in boots. And besides, if they didn't spot us crossing that flat yonder in the moonlight they'd track us down in the mud in no time."

"They'll guard the barn!" she whispered fearfully. "We can't get horses. Our only hope is the ravine. Then we can work along under the bank to Powder River. It's less than a mile."

"Less than a mile?" he asked, his own endless experience in the hailstorm recurring vividly. He started on a dog trot across the flat beside her. "If I didn't walk twenty miles I didn't walk a foot. You've got me guessing. First off I meet you telling fortunes with a carnival company. You warn me to keep my eye peeled for a dark gent. I've tied up with two already. Ed Jackson and this Keller. Then you tell Mournful he's got occult power. What does he do but drive me plumb crazy with his hunches."

"Mournful, as you call him, doesn't have very many of those hunches that don't come true!" she threw at him, quickening her pace as a light flared up in the house and an angry shout announced that Keller had been released from his fetters. "And besides, he's the best friend you have on earth." Before he could answer her she sprinted for the ravine. He lumbered along awkwardly in his high-heeled boots. But for all his effort he did not catch up with her again until she had jumped over the rim. Side by side they sat down on the rain-soaked ground to get their breath.

"I'm not saying Mournful isn't the best friend I've got," Happy returned when he could talk. "But he's played hunches till he's got me to worrying—something I've never did before in my life—and now I stray into this Circle H outfit, half beaten to death with hail, and get shot and meet you. You say Keller took you prisoner and you're r'aring to escape from him or somebody else. Who, you either can't or won't tell. What's it all about, anyhow?" He pierced her with an inquisitive gaze.

She raised up cautiously, peered across the flat. "They've gotten their horses and are leaving the corral! Quick!" was her answer in a jerky tone. "They'll track us in no time."

Keeping well under shelter of the bank, she started up the ravine.

"I had a hunch they would," he said when he had overtaken her again. Mournful's pet expression on his own lips filled him with dismay. "I told you so," he corrected himself only to find that again he had unconsciously quoted Mournful. “Let them come!” he flared in desperation. “I’ll—”

“You’ll do nothing of the kind!” she flashed with spirit. “We’re going to beat them to the river—right up this draw.”

“What are you going to do when you get there?” he panted, trying gamely to maintain the swift pace she set.

“Swim it, if we have to. Anything to get away from Keller.”

“Swim Powder River—at flood stage just to get away from that four-flusher and a few men?” he snorted. “Listen, Miss, I’d rather save my wind and tie into the whole bunch.”

“You’ll have a mighty good chance if they catch us,” she returned grimly. “It isn’t far to the river now.”

“You sure know this country like a book for a fortune-teller,” he observed, shooting her a sidelong glance in the darkness. “Is your occult power working?”

“It doesn’t take occult power to know where the river is,” she threw back angrily. “Can’t you hear it?”

He stopped, breathless, for a moment. Ahead he caught the boom and crash of angry water. With a start he recalled his first glimpse of the river when the pony he had taken from Keller had paused on the very brink of its cañon and it had been revealed to him by flashes of lightning just before the hailstorm. Involuntarily he shuddered. He turned to the girl. But she was looking back at their pursuers who, plainly visible in the moonlight, had started across the flat, their mounts making slow progress in the slippery gumbo.

"Reckon it's best to hide out in the brakes till daylight," he wheezed. "There isn't any use in risking our lives jumping into that river at night."

"I won't unless I have to," she told him. "But I'll do it before either one of us goes back to the Circle H with Keller. If it isn't too high yet we'd better do it tonight before it comes up higher with the storm. I've got to get across by tomorrow."

"What for?" he demanded. "Is there somebody over there you want to see?"

"Yes!"

"Who?"

"Clee Davis."

"Mournful?" He stopped in his tracks, puffing violently. "He didn't get across ahead of the storm. Why it was ten miles from where—"

"No it wasn't," she interrupted, seizing him by the arm and pulling him along in the shadow of the bank to escape detection by Keller and his men, who now were pounding so close they could hear the thud of their horses' hoofs. "It was a scant two miles from where you . . ." She paused for an instant. ". . . From where you stopped this afternoon."

"Keller, the dirty liar, told us it was fifteen," he blurted out, apparently not noticing her hesitation. "What do you suppose his object was in lying? Say, if you've been a prisoner back there like you claim, what do you know about my herd?"

"I wasn't a prisoner until after—after I'd helped Mournful point the herd across the river," she returned, speeding up. "Keller caught me just as the storm broke!"

"Well, I'll be damned!" he growled ungallantly. "Who in the devil are you anyway? What have you got to meet Mournful in such a rush for?"

"Do you see those shadowed brakes right over there?" She evaded his question and pointed ahead. "We've got to make them. Then we'll be safe. We can climb the bluffs under cover."

"I'm thankful the herd is all right," he groaned, striving valiantly to follow her in a spirit that drained his ebbing strength. "But I'll sure give Mournful a piece of my mind for doing his courting when he's got a thousand critters to look out for. Of course, he isn't to blame, though, if a girl is crazy enough about him to swim—"

"Don't be an idiot, H—Happy Day," she cut in severely, faltering on his name. "Save your breath and run!"

CHAPTER XVI

The next few minutes were a nightmare to Happy Day. Utterly fatigued as he had been at the start of the race it now seemed that he never could hold out to reach the brakes, which loomed dark and foreboding before them. The breath tore at his lungs, rasped croupily in his dry throat. His head was light, spinning with hunger and exertion. The awful battering he had endured during the storm left him spent and helpless. He could scarcely summon strength to lift the mud-caked boots that hung like leaden shackles about his legs and feet. Now, almost within gun-shot pounded Keller and his crew. . . . So close Happy could hear the curses of the gang, the whistling snorts of the unshod horses as they slid about in the sticky, popping gumbo.

Then of a sudden all the punishment he had endured centered in one horrible moment. "I can't make it!" he managed to gasp out. "You go ahead. I'll hold them off."

"No! No!" Goldie cried. "You must come. It isn't more than a hundred yards. Hang on. . . . Here!"

Throwing her arm about him, she attempted to help him along. But he shook her off impatiently. "I'll make it alone," he mumbled gamely, reeling on. ". . . or not at all. But if I just knew what the devil we're running for I'd . . ." He could get no farther. He stopped again, fighting savagely for breath. She waited, her nervous gaze whipping the flats behind. Again he took a grip on himself, staggered on. The last few steps to a yawning crevice in the bluffs he made groping like a blind man, finally to throw himself full length on the ground, deep in the gloom of the refuge.

"Rest for a minute, Happy," she panted, seating herself beside him. "It was a shame to ask you to make a run like that, tired as you were. Cowboys can't run for sour grapes at the best; but you're game to try."

Her encouragement seemed to give him new life. When he had succeeded in getting some control over his rasping breath, he raised up to peer at her inquiringly through the darkness. "Where next?" he gasped.

"Up," she replied quickly. "They'll track us here in a few more minutes. By going up the crevice we can stay out of gun-shot in the shadows. It isn't far. Can you make it?"

"Light out!" he whispered. "I don't know what it's all about, but as long as I'm into it I might as well keep going."

Slipping, clawing in the slippery gumbo for a foothold she finally succeeded in ascending the first pitch from where the crevice rose gradually to the top of the bluff. With difficulty he followed the agile girl. Yet while the climb was a stiff one, it seemed to ease his legs, which had become numb with the fatigue of running under the handicap of high heels. She was waiting above to lend a hand when he came puffing up over the rim of the pitch.

"Now we can rest for a while," she said almost gaily. "They can't see us up here, and they can't follow us on horseback. If they shoot we have a good breastwork."

"Shoot," he snorted. "They wouldn't shoot at a girl."

"You don't know that bunch like I do," she flashed. "They'd do anything. But save your wind, Happy. We'll be—" Her voice trailed off. "Why, what's become of them?" she whispered anxiously. "They ought to be at the crevice by now. Can you hear them?"

He tried to hear above the pounding blood in his straining ears. But the only sound was a sluicing roar, the thumping of his own heart. "Mebbyso they got discouraged and gave up the chase, figuring they couldn't find us in the brakes."

"Not Keller," she said grimly. "He's too tricky. How do you feel now?"

"Oh, I'm all right now," he replied carelessly. "Just winded."

"Can you go on to the top?"

"Sure. But you're a danged sight safer here. What do you want to go up there for?"

She did not wait to answer. Springing lightly to her feet she darted away in the shadows. Getting up stiffly he plunged after her.

The heart-breaking trip to the crown of the bluff was made without incident and in silence save for their rasping breath and the occasional thud of gumbo dislodged by groping feet. The girl was waiting when Happy pulled himself up.

"It's about two hundred yards east to an old ford on Powder River," she whispered. "The bank has crumbled away and it isn't very high. We can make it easily. See, the river isn't up—yet."

He looked below. Glinting in the moonlight was the mighty Powder. Sight of it was not half so terrifying as when he had seen it boiling up in the lightning-riddled darkness. But with the instinct of a man of the plains, unaccustomed to large bodies of water, he eyed it suspiciously. Puzzled by the strange turn things had taken, he still asked no question when she arose presently and without a word started along the top of the bluff.

In silence he followed; in silence they gained the ford. Thankful that at last he could rest he followed her down a slippery slope.

"Here we are!" she announced. "It's only a couple of hundred feet across here and not very deep. Now we can wait, until daylight. Then if—" A scream escaped her. All about them men were springing up. "Quick Happy!" she whispered. "We'll have to swim it!"

"Not tonight, you won't!" came the rumbling voice of Keller from the bank directly in front of them. "I out-figured you, didn't I, cutie? You don't happen to be the only one who knows about this ford. You thought we were still down there tracking you at the foot of the bluffs, didn't you? But we took a short cut. Here we are. And you're going back with us." He loomed huge in the moonlight, which glinted on his blue-barreled forty-five trained on Happy, who had stopped dead in his tracks to stand immobile as stone. "I ought to kill you for helping this girl get away!" he snarled. "You've given me the slip twice—but this time you're not going to. You're under arrest for horse stealing, defying the law and for rustling!"

Strangely the words Keller hurled at him did not roil Happy half so much as the fact that the fellow had addressed Goldie as cutie. His first inclination was to leap forward, swing on the swollen, leering face revealed now in startling detail by the bright moonlight flooding the bench above the river on which they stood. But he quickly realized the folly of such a move. Even if he did succeed in knocking Keller down, before he could draw, the others would riddle them with lead. It was not of himself he was thinking. Since he had encountered the girl at the Circle H, he had come to feel a sense of guardianship, although, he admitted reluctantly, it had been she who had led the way.

"All right, Keller," he said presently, in such a tone of complete surrender as to bring a gasp from Goldie. "I reckon you got me dead to rights this time. Where are you going to take me?"

"Back to the ranch," Keller growled, plainly surprised at Happy's sudden docility. "One of you jaspers fetch up the horses!" he ordered his men. "It looks like we've showed this walloper where to head in at. Throw down your forty-five fellow!" he shot at Happy. Happy's movements were slow and deliberate. But his mind was working like lightning. By now the men had closed in—five of them, counting Keller. He swept them in a single glance, recognizing them as part of the crew the stock inspector had had with him on the trail.

"Well, hustle up!" Keller exploded. "Get rid of that gun of yours or . . ."

From the corner of his eye, Happy watched the puncher moving away toward the top of the bluff after the horses. The girl he knew was directly behind him. He sensed her nearness, imagined he could feel her breath on his neck.

The scheme he had hit upon in his desperation was so utterly simple it seemed impossible of . . .

"My God, look!" he cried suddenly.

The ruse worked beyond his wildest hope. To a man the gang wheeled to see what misfortune had overtaken their companion. In a flash Happy went for his forty-five. It seemed to leap to meet his hand. He sprang away, shielding Goldie with his body.

"Now you simple-minded wallopers, throw down your own guns!" he chuckled. "Two can play at this game."

Nonplused at being caught off their guard, the group dropped their weapons to the ground. All but Keller. His Colt spat savagely. The bullet whined a song of hate past Happy's ear. Happy's finger contracted on the trigger. But foe that Keller was he could not . . .

"I don't want to kill you, Keller!" he flung out through set teeth. "So I'm still giving you one more chance. Throw down that gun."

Keller's only answer was to fire again. Point blank. But this time two reports boomed through the cañon. Keller's gun went flying from his hand. The big fellow went lurching back, clutching at his wrist, bawling curses. Then it seemed that he lost his head completely. Roaring like a bull, he charged Happy. Loathe to kill him, Happy side-stepped to let him pass.

"Stay behind me, Goldie!" he whispered hoarsely to the girl. "If I have to plug him I will. . . . But I don't want to, especially while you're here. Have you got a gun?"

"Yes!" The low voice that came back to him was amazingly cool. "And they're covered!"

Just then Keller wheeled and came back. On the lower side of the incline now, before Happy could swing, he lost his footing, went down on one knee. Keller fell upon him, bearing him to the ground with such force as to drive the breath from his lungs. For an instant he lay gasping. Then, bridging he rolled the clumsy, wounded fellow off and leaped to his feet.

Again Keller came up and charged. Happy stepped back to meet him with the blow that twice before had knocked him out. He heard Goldie scream a warning. Before he realized her meaning the slippery bank crumbled beneath his foot. He was conscious of a sickening, horrible sensation. . . . He was hurtling backwards into the river! He struck the water sprawled on his back. Half winded by the impact he went under, came to the surface fighting for air.

"Save him! Save him!" Goldie was crying to the motionless crew.

"Save him nothing, cutie!" Keller's coarse laugh came to Happy. "Let the lousy rustler drown—that's what he gets for trying to kidnap you. . . . Here, where you going?"

"To save him myself!" she cried scornfully.

"Like the devil you are," Keller roared, springing toward her, only to recoil at sight of the gun in her hand. "You're going back. . . ."

"Not this time, Keller!" she taunted. "But don't forget, we'll meet again!"

Wondering what she meant, thrilled by her utter fearlessness, his nerves tingling with the realization that she was willing to risk her life in an attempt to save him, Happy tried to shout to her that he was all right, warn her to hold the crew at bay until he could scout the bank for a place to land. But before he could spew the muddy water from his mouth she had backed to the edge of the bank. An oath left Keller's lips. He sprang forward. Goldie wheeled, poised for a moment, a trim figure silhouetted in the moonlight, then dove. She struck the water almost beside him.

"Happy! Happy!" she called softly, coming to the surface. "Where are you?"

"Here!" he answered through teeth already chattering with cold. "It's mighty brave of—"

"It's no time for compliments!" she said sharply. "Swim! They'll shoot!"

Treading water while he yanked off his boots and unbuckling his cartridge belt and chaps he kicked out of them and started after her just as a volley from the bank splattered lead on the water about them.

"Dive!" she ordered tersely, disappearing from sight.

CHAPTER XVII

Never more than a swimmer of mediocre ability, before he could pull from range of the belching Colts on the bank, Happy was forced to tax his already wasted strength to the utmost. Time and again his clumsy diving took him down to the swift undertow, from which he was able to free himself with only a desperate struggle. When he no longer could hear the crack of the forty-fives above the pounding in his ears, he shook the water from his eyes and looked around for the girl. He located her presently, directly ahead, swimming slightly upstream and apparently calculating the distance the current would carry them to the crossing below. He could not but admire the graceful ease with which she breasted the rushing river. Came to him a momentary wonder if there was anything she was incapable of doing and doing well. But he had no time for idle thoughts. The task at hand he knew, would drain both his mental and physical strength to the lowest ebb.

"Are you sure you know where you're going?" he managed to shout.

Her only answer was to raise one arm from the water and beckon him on. He strove to keep up with her but he could only flounder along awkwardly, while she seemed to be experiencing little or no difficulty with the strong current.

He dared a glance backwards. Apparently Keller and his men had left the bank for he could see nothing of them. . . . Only the ugly black bluffs rearing up, sinister and ominous in the moonlight.

After a considerable time, during which he fought doggedly with the undertow sucking at his legs, the freezing cold that was seeping to the marrow of his bones, and a throbbing pain in the slight flesh wound on his arm, they reached the center of the stream. He could make out the outline of the opposite shore glinting like a ribbon of silver at the base of high bluffs. With a mighty effort he drew alongside of the girl.

"Where do we head in?" he shouted.

"See . . . Where the water is eddying at the point of the highest bluff!" came her reply.

"The current seems to be getting stronger!" he cried.

"And colder!" she threw back. "I'm nearly frozen. Besides the river is rising terribly fast. . . . Can't you notice it. . . . We've got to hurry."

"We're going to hit below that bluff!" he observed, swimming for all he was worth. "Unless—"

A sinister hiss that drowned out his voice sent his gaze whipping upstream. The blood seemed to freeze in his veins. Billowing down upon them were the headwaters of the flood! He tried to shout a warning to Goldie. It died on his lips. The seething, foaming water burst over him in a deluge. Choking, clawing, fighting, he was tossed bodily into the air. He fell back only to be sucked below the surface. Endless moments of frantic struggles passed before he could wrench himself from the awful undertow and rise. Then he looked around for the girl. She had disappeared!

He attempted to tread water while he scanned the moonlit river, which, in a twinkling, had become an angry, snarling torrent, the strength of its current increased until it defied his sturdiest efforts, and spun him about like a chip on a whirlpool.

Then, of a sudden, he saw her head bob to the surface downstream. Forgetful of everything except that this girl, who had risked her own life for him would drown unless he could rescue her, he threw caution to the winds and flung himself headlong after her. Aided by the terrific flood wash, he quickly caught her, seized hold of her clothing. The added weight momentarily checked his precipitate course. Hanging on to her grimly, he mustered all the strength at his command to tear her from the grasp of the undertow. Presently he succeeded in raising her head above the surface. She lay like dead in his arms.

Minutes passed; heart-breaking minutes when

he could have sobbed with his pitiful impotence to combat the treacherous river, which seemed to roar its derision of his puny efforts.

He swept the moonlit bank, striving the while to keep both their heads above water. With sinking heart he found that they had been carried past the ford the girl had pointed out. Everywhere the towering bluffs seemed to rise sheer from the water's edge. The discovery descended upon him with the weight of a crushing blow. For the first time in his life he was tempted to give up—bruised, aching, beaten!

The girl shifted slightly in his arms.

"Where—am—I?" she gasped out through teeth chattering with cold.

"In the middle of Powder River," he panted. "We missed the ford."

He could feel her body go rigid. "A piece of driftwood—stunned—me!" she choked. "Let—me—go!"

Reluctant to release her lest she be sucked under again, he clung to her. But she jerked away from him.

"I'm—all—right!" she faltered painfully. "Drift—down—stream. Another—ford—two—miles!" Before he could stop her she was gone.

Grateful to be rid of her weight, yet torn with anxiety for her safety, he surrendered himself to the swift current. They shot along at sickening speed. Through half-closed eyes Happy caught occasional glimpses of the moonlit heavens. It was almost as light as day on top the bluffs that now towered above them like colossal, eerie monsters. From time to time he raised his head to watch the girl. But apparently she had recovered, for she was riding the surface far more buoyantly than he himself.

"Happy!" her voice came back to him. "The ford! Right below! Here!"

The last was a scream of despair. Before they could tear away from the treacherous current they were being swept past the second landing! Below he could hear a dull roar.

"What's that?" he shouted.

"The rapids!" There was stark terror in her voice. "We've got to land here or be killed!"

He floundered alongside of her, lending what aid he could to tear her from the current and toward the ford, a foam-crested whirlpool just outside the torrent.

With a strength born of desperation he met the current head on, going under the surface in an effort to fight his way upstream. After several futile attempts he succeeded in lunging to a point a little above the landing.

"Can you hold your own for a few seconds?" he panted grimly. "Till I catch some wind."

"I'll—try," she responded gamely.

Releasing her, he measured the distance from where a dim cowtrail entered the water to where the girl was fighting stubbornly. In a glance he calculated it to be fifty feet. Too far to attempt to carry her . . . Too far for her to go on her own wasted strength. Alone he was confident he could make it. But—

"Go on, Happy!" she cried. "Save yourself. It's your last chance. If—"

At that moment her strength deserted her. But before she could go under he seized hold of her again.

Then began the struggle of Happy's life; a terrific, maddening struggle that brought stinging tears to his eyes and strained his muscles cruelly; that, time and again, sapped his strength until he had to clench his teeth on the pains that racked his body. For one thing he was thankful. The girl was in full possession of her faculties—serious as was their predicament never once did she lose her head.

After an infinity of time, during which the roar of the falls below seemed to grow infernally loud, he succeeded in fighting his way with her to a place where he found he could touch bottom, although the dirty water swirled about his neck and kept him swaying like a cork.

"Now!" he panted. "Give me your feet." Reaching down he clutched her about the ankles.

"Put what you've got into every stroke," he commanded, spewing out a mouthful of muddy water. "Swim straight for the landing. I'm going to give you a shove. . . . Keep your legs stiff. . . . Push against me."

He waited a minute until he was in a position to bundle every muscle.

"Now!"

He could feel the girl's body starting away from him. With a tremendous effort, he pushed. She shot into the whirlpool. . . . A moment of wild churning . . . A glad cry burst on his ears. She straightened up in the water, threw herself headlong onto the bank.

He stood for a second trying to regain his balance. The undertow sucked tenaciously at his feet. The current was too strong for him to hurl himself forward. Inch by inch he was being tipped backwards. He tried to roll on his side. Herculean hands were holding him upright while some gigantic force was impelling him backwards! He fell to floundering wildly. Then, for all he could do, he felt himself going down, down.

On the verge of collapse the undertow released him. He rose to the surface, fought frantically for breath. The roar of the rapids crashed on his ears. He tried to swim. His efforts were to no avail. Louder and louder grew the roar. Minutes were eternities. No longer did he have the strength nor the will to resist. It was a hopeless, losing fight. He found himself praying that it would end quickly. He closed his eyes, waiting for the plunge that would send him hurtling on to the rocks below. In the fleeting seconds he tried to picture the wild tumult into which he would land.

Then he was hurled against a solid object. Instinctively he clutched it, clung until his bloodless hands were numb with the pressure. With a strength born of sheer desperation he pulled himself closer and looked around. He had been thrown against a ragged rock of considerable size. About him swirled the foaming yellow water. The undertow suddenly seemed to increase a thousand-fold. Despite his frantic efforts it was again sucking him down, tearing loose his grip on the slippery rock.

With almost a superhuman effort he wrenched his legs from the deadly tentacles. Inch by inch he worked his way up the rock, finally dragging his leaden feet from the water and throwing himself flat on its slippery surface. A wave of nausea swept over him. The deafening roar of the rapids suddenly became a throb in the distance. He lay shivering, clinging for dear life to the rock; fighting gamely against a mantle of darkness that flapped, wraith-like, before his aching eyes.

CHAPTER XVIII

The moon was a great yellow ball hanging directly over the cañon of Powder River when Happy Day roused from the coma of collapse. His first conscious thought was of the flood water that beat a terrific tattoo in his popping ears. He was shivering violently. His teeth had chattered until his jaws hurt. His soaked clothing, stiff with cold, clung like a coating of ice to his cramped and aching body.

When he was able to force his logy muscles to do his will, he pulled himself painfully to a sitting posture on the rock, which, although little more than large enough to accommodate him, projected several feet above the water. He fumbled in his pocket for a cigaret. He found both tobacco and papers, but they were hopelessly water-soaked. Cursing his luck he looked around.

As his thoughts took order he forgot his own predicament. His one fear suddenly was for Goldie. His eyes flew upstream, strove to penetrate the deep gloom that transformed the cañon walls into ominous, shadowy monsters. A towering bluff, around which the river—the color of old gold in the moonlight—made a sharp bend, hid from sight the landing where he believed he had last seen her. Bitter disappointment assailed him. While he was positive that she had escaped death in the flood he was not so sure she had survived the cold and exposure.

He shouted several times. The only answer was the echo of his own voice battering to whispers on the cañon walls and the angry roar of the muddy water. Prey to haunting fear that even now she might be in desperate need of his help, he began to take hurried stock of his surroundings.

His refuge, he discovered, was almost in the center of a chain of rocks that extended to the far bank, forming a bridge which, with great care could be crossed. A slip however, meant a plunge into the rapids fifty feet below. He watched, with terrible fascination, the water tumbling about him to run smooth as glass for a distance then hurl itself against the jagged rocks and be dashed to spray. With a shudder he offered silent thanks for deliverance from the awful doom.

When his ears had become accustomed to the infernal roar and his spinning head had quieted, he felt more secure on his dizzy perch. He began swinging his arms to speed up sluggish circulation. The exercise soon warmed the blood in his frozen veins. Getting to his feet warily he straightened up to stand for several seconds looking back and forth across the river.

"Well, I'll be damned!" he exclaimed in bewilderment. "I can only get out on the side of the river I fell in—and Goldie's on the other side."

The more he pondered the thing the more puzzled he became. The shadowed banks were identical but there was no crossing over. Determined however, not to remain any longer than need be on the freezing refuge if, indeed, he could quit it without undue risk, he chose the only route which offered access to shore and measured the distance to the nearest rock with his eyes. When he was confident he could make it in safety he bundled his muscles and leaped—a panicky moment in the air—then he landed squarely upon the rock, clinging frantically. Pausing long enough to catch his breath and make sure of himself, he went on to the next.

It was almost a half hour later when, panting and weary, he dragged himself onto a ledge at the foot of the bluffs and sat down to catch the breath that rasped in his throat.

Presently he became aware that the shadows about him were deepening. He glanced apprehensively at the strip of star-lit sky far above. The moon had dropped from sight over the rim of the bluffs. Stygian darkness, made more horrible by the deafening roar of the rapids, was swiftly enveloping the cañon. The chill again began to creep into his bones. Awful as it had been in a wane light, in darkness . . . With sinking heart he realized that there was nothing now to do but wait for daylight.

Cursing the delay, he sat hunched up, striving

to pierce the gloom, until the cold became unbearable. Then in desperation he stretched himself flat and wormed his way along to explore the ledge, hoping that in spite of the darkness he could find some way out of the predicament. He had gone but a short distance when the shelf narrowed until he could advance no farther without plunging into the water.

Moving backwards until he could turn around, he crawled in the opposite direction. Here too he encountered an insurmountable barrier. The ledge came to an abrupt end directly over the rapids!

"Damn!" he muttered savagely, getting to his feet and bracing himself against the bluff to keep from losing his wits in the turmoil. "I'm in a pretty fix. . . . Wonder if I could swim to that other side? Wish morning would come so I could get head or tail to this cañon—it's sure just plenty lonesome down here by myself. I reckon there is nothing to do but shag around to keep warm until it is light enough to see something."

With that he started pacing the length of the shelf, cursing the ill-fortune that held him a prisoner until daylight should reveal some way out. As he stamped about in his sock feet, thankful at least for the exercise that warmed him to some extent, the events since his arrival in the badlands began stalking before him. Things had happened with such amazing rapidity that he found difficulty in getting them straight in his mind. The stampede of the strange herd, Keller's sudden appearance and Mournful's lies puzzled him deeply.

"Damn that Mournful," he said aloud, starting at the echo of his own voice slapping back at him from out of the darkness. "If he had just kept those hunches to himself and told the truth! What the devil was his object in telling Keller the boss's name was Jack Halliday and that he'd gone up the trail, anyhow? What did he mean when he said nobody would find those strays in the herd?"

With ample time to mull over the affair he found that the motives which had prompted the *segundo*'s strange actions were as far beyond his comprehension now as ever.

"Wonder why Goldie was so dead anxious to meet that hunch-playing old codger tomorrow?" he mused on. "She said she helped him point the herd across the river ahead of the storm. What in the name of blazes does a pretty little thing like her see in that duffer? He's old enough to be her father!"

Here again was something beyond his ken. And any thought of the girl disturbed him greatly, brought the old fear for her safety flaring up anew. Yet even had he known where she was he was powerless to get to her in the darkness.

Questions concerning her, questions that he had had no time to ponder until now, started tumbling through his mind. What was she doing on Powder River? Why had she been so secretive about herself? Why had she been on the trail alone before the storm? Why had she been taken to the Circle H—a prisoner? He could scarcely bring himself to believe that Keller, a stock inspector, for all his devilishness, would dare abduct her as she claimed. Yet, when Keller had surprised them on the river bluff as they were making their escape, he had told her that she was going back with him.

Who was the stranger she had warned him was returning to the ranch with Keller's men, who had gone down the trail after the storm? Why, when she apparently knew the Powder River country so well, didn't she know who owned the Circle H? What had she meant when she said she was trying to find out? And why had she been so insistent that he quit the Circle H with her when by remaining he could have rested, held Keller at bay until daylight, then overtaken his herd? At the moment the whole affair smacked strongly of melodrama; a poor attempt to make mystery out of a few chance happenings which, while they seemed to fulfil Mournful's gloomy predictions, could scarcely be anything more than a series of unfortunate coincidences.

Hot anger against the girl took possession of him. "She isn't anything but a calamity-howler—just like Mournful!" he snorted disgustedly. "Just four-flushing again, like she was at Halfway when she told me a dark man was coming into my life. I didn't believe her then and I don't believe her now. But why was I fool enough to listen to her, follow her on this wild goose chase just because she claimed she wanted to give Keller the slip and get to Mournful? The whole damned thing looks fishy—her and all the rest of this horse play!

"You poor fool!" he chided himself bitterly in the next breath. "You're losing your head over that filly." He jerked back against the side wall. "You come nigh onto walking off this ledge into the water just thinking about her. . . . She's stuck on Mournful. A fine chance you'd have of beating his time—even if you wanted to."

Yet the anger, that was boiling up within him, cooled with a mental picture of Goldie holding the crew at bay on the bluffs above the river while he battled Keller. Then he saw her poised, ready for the dive; risking her life for him. But he was robbed of the thrill it gave him by another thought. She had wanted to cross the river anyway—to see Mournful! His jaws clicked grimly. He tried to cast her from his mind. But the haunting memory of that final struggle in the flood, his last glimpse of her, persisted.

His thoughts, now running riot, flew on to the herd. Ed Jackson's predictions that he would never take it through to summer range and back to the Rocking Chair ranch seemed to be coming true. Thus far he had done no better than Jackson who, in this very region the previous spring, had lost the thousand head entrusted to his care. Here he was, the night of their arrival at Powder River, marooned, bootless, half frozen and unarmed, in the cañon of the river, his cattle somewhere in the badlands and with no possible chance of overtaking them for hours to come. A groan escaped him. After his trouble with Jackson, and for all the confidence the Old Man had imposed in him by making him trail boss of the Rocking Chair, it seemed that he was destined to do exactly what Jackson had done—lose his herd.

Only now it was worse. He was guilty of a thing no cowman would believe. He was lost from his herd! And all because of his willingness to heed the pleas of a pretty girl who might, for all he knew, have been leading him on deliberately.

With an effort he dismissed the whole affair from his mind, resolved first to get out of the cañon, then find the herd and stick with it day and night until it returned to the Rocking Chair.

After an infinity of time the stars began to brighten. Predawn darkness blotted out the cañon walls. He paused in his pacing to squat on his heels and stare so long and hard into the stygian blackness that flares of light set to dancing before his sightless gaze. Chafing under delay, his nerves frayed from the incessant roar of the rapids, his body shaking violently with cold, he waited.

Hours later a faint light began to rout the stars and creep into the cañon. He watched it with fascination. First a drab gray, then tinges of pink, red and green. A splash of fire-yellow—a panorama of changing color.

Yet with dawn the shadows only seemed to deepen about him. Instead of warmth daylight made it colder. Then the light from a brilliant sun etched a line just below the rim of the opposite gumbo bluffs. Lower and lower it came, dispelling the gloom and drawing a sparkling mist from the booming river.

As quickly as he could see he arose and began a study of his surroundings. The ledge on which he stood was but twice the width of his body and some twenty feet long. The bluffs rose precipitately above him, their crumbling, corrugated sides impossible of ascent. To scale the walls on the opposite shore would be, if possible, even more difficult. The increasing light revealed clearly the utter hopelessness of his position. He was trapped. And much as he dreaded it, his one hope of escape lay in again taking to the river.

He stared into the muddy water, which was receding slowly, leaving a rim of muck and slime on the rocks above the rapids.

"It's got to be done," he decided grimly. "The

sooner I do it the quicker I'll find . . ." It was on the tip of his tongue to mention the girl and not the herd, which had been entrusted to his care.

"Damn!" he exclaimed. "What did she want to be at the Circle H for when the hailstorm drove me in there? If it hadn't been for her I wouldn't be here like this!"

Unwilling to admit to himself that he would find her if he could before he attempted to overtake the herd, he glanced again into the river and shuddered. Then he looked up the stream. Around the point of the bluff might be the ford where she had landed. Even now she might be lying there unconscious and half frozen!

Anxiety drove him to slip a foot gingerly in the water.

"B-r-r!" He shivered. "It's cold! No wonder I got chilly last night. I'll bet they cut ice on this damned river in the middle of July."

Gritting his teeth, he edged further in. His foot slid down a steep incline of gumbo, then touched rock bottom. Cautiously he eased in his other foot and stood upright. The water caught him around the waist. But so near the shore it lacked the swift undercurrent that had come so close to sealing his doom the night before.

Hugging the bank, and careful to secure a hand hold before taking another step, he moved slowly away from the rapids. Gaining the bluff, he peered anxiously around it. As he had half expected, a few rods above was a shallow eddy from which a cowtrail wandered away toward a crevice in the steep cañon walls. But Goldie was nowhere in sight!

His pace quickened. He reached the ford without accident. Dragging himself ashore, he made a hasty survey of the ground. Apparently nothing had left the river at that point in years for there was not a single track.

More disappointed than he would even admit to himself at not finding some trace of the girl, he turned his back on the river and made off up the trail. Reaching the crevice, he began the laborious ascent, now dropping on all fours to crawl around a narrow shelf overhanging the river, again clambering breathlessly over great, shifting piles of crushed gumbo. Panting and weary, he came at last to the top of the bluff. Eagerly he pulled himself over the rim and looked around!

CHAPTER XIX

If Happy had held any hope of catching sight of either the girl or the big Rocking Chair herd from the top of the river bluff he was doomed to disappointment. Getting slowly to his feet, he swept the country, which spread out in a vast panorama before him. Below glinted the river, muddy and ugly in the light of day, flanked by towering palisades. Beyond, fantastically-shaped buttes reared their heads from the coulée-gashed floor of the badlands. When his eyes had begun to water from vainly searching the wastes for a glimpse of the herd he turned to look in the opposite direction.

It was but a continuation of the monotonous stretches, drab and colorless, the pinnacles constantly changing contour in the heat haze which, early as it was, shimmered upward from the cracked gumbo. Still he saw no movement that could be the herd. . . . Only an illimitable sweep of desolation, utterly devoid of life.

He glanced at the blinding sun, then toward the west. He turned slowly in all directions.

"Dang it all, I'm still on the side of the river I started from!" he exclaimed. "If I only could have crossed those rocks above the rapids some other way!" He continued to gaze about ponderingly.

"And if Goldie is alive—she's over yonder!" He looked across the river. "I'm a fine jasper at helping a girl! Well," he muttered grimly to himself, "I can't stay here all my life! It's a cinch I'm not going back down there to swim that river, so I'll just light out and see if I can find a ranch. I've got to rustle something to eat and drink before I locate the herd."

He ran his gaze along the top of the bluffs—some quarter of a mile in width—which stretched away, level as a floor, to meet the horizon.

"Reckon it doesn't make much difference what way I go," he mused. "Just so I go somewhere."

For no reason other than to keep the blistering sun out of his eyes he started northward, limping along painfully, picking his way cautiously through the scattered bunches of cactus and detouring the clumps of greasewood and yucca.

As the morning advanced the heat increased. Where he had been cold during the night he now was burning hot, the sweat trickling across his face. The wound in his arm throbbed painfully. His unshod feet were blistered and sore. The pangs of hunger gnawed constantly at his stomach. His thirst became almost unbearable. When he had reached a point where he felt he no longer could go on, he threw himself flat on the ground to stare out over the country. A few minutes of idle survey and he started up. Directly below, a mile or more from the foot of the bluff, was a ranch-house.

"Reckon I'm getting lucky again!" he cried happily. "Here's where I put on the nose bag, borrow a horse and some boots and catch up with the herd."

Running to the rim of the bluff, he scouted around until he located a place where he could descend. With reckless haste he went down the side. Dropping into a wide ravine at the bottom he went forward as swiftly as he could, vaguely conscious of something familiar in the surroundings, yet too hungry and thirsty to give them any attention. Mounting the bank of the draw, he took a short cut across a big flat toward the ranch, now plainly visible.

As he came nearer a feeling that he had seen the ranch itself before assailed him. Completely at a loss to account for the haunting sense of familiarity sight of the place stirred within him, he fell to studying it closely as he approached. There was nothing about the rambling log barn with its sod roof, the small horse pasture beyond—in which grazed a cavvy of some twenty head—the bunkhouses or the sheds that was different from any other ranch he had seen. He was positive that he had never laid eyes on any of them before. It was the ranch-house, a two-story log structure, that was familiar, he decided.

Still he went on, prey to vague misgivings.

Mounting a rise suddenly, he sighted a bunch of horsemen grouped about the round corrals below the barn. A cloud of dust and uproarious shouts told him that somebody was fighting an outlaw inside the enclosure. After the lonely experiences of the past few hours the noise and thought of companionship were decidedly welcome. He quickened his pace only to stop dead in his tracks almost within hailing distance of the group at the corral.

"Hell!" he blurted out. "No wonder that house looked familiar. This spread is the Circle H or I'm as crazy as a locoed steer!"

The thing seemed so utterly improbable it dumfounded him. He stared about in amazement. Yet there were the tracks left by the girl and himself, along with those of several horses, crossing the flat toward the ravine down which he had just come. They were evidence conclusive. Small wonder things had seemed familiar! Fate had tricked him back to the Circle H, the one place in the entire Powder River country where he could expect nothing.

He hesitated, fighting stubbornly against the gnawing pains in his stomach—which pleaded with him to go on—undecided whether to risk capture by Keller or detour the ranch, pick up the trail of his own herd and endure the hunger and thirst until he could overtake it.

As he paused, a broad-shouldered man strode

toward the corrals. Happy watched him closely. It was not Keller. Yet there was something familiar about the fellow. His loose-hipped gait, the way he had of swinging his arms reminded him strangely of someone he had known. But for the life of him he could not tell who.

Reaching the corrals, the stranger untied the bridle reins of a saddled pony and swung up. Pausing only long enough to speak to the horsemen idling about, he roweled from sight behind the house, followed by the entire group save one who remained behind inside the corral. Crouching, Happy waited. Presently the party appeared below, let down a gate and galloped away toward the east, heading directly for a wide gap in the river bluffs some two miles distant. The sun glistening on water just beyond the gap revealed to Happy for the first time the ford where Mournful, no doubt, had crossed Powder River with the Rocking Chair herd.

When he was reasonably certain that the horsemen would not return immediately, Happy's eyes flew back to the corral. But apparently the man within was having no success in mounting the saddled outlaw—if, indeed, he was attempting to do more than halter and saddle-break it—for it only backed around the corral and snorted and squealed so savagely that many of the cavvy ponies in the nearby horse pasture stopped grazing to come up, hang their heads over the top strand of barbed-wire and stare inquisitively at the strange proceedings.

Dragging the outlaw up to the poles presently, the fellow tied it securely and crawled out of the corral, slapping the dust from his shirt and chaps. The sunlight glittered on silver conchas. One arm was bandaged. Happy's nerves sang with tautness. It was Keller. But evidently the inspector had not noticed him for he went directly to the house and disappeared.

Determined now that the others had left, to eat, drink, secure boots, a firearm and a mount even if he was forced to fight Keller a third time, Happy started ahead stealthily. He had taken but a few steps when he stopped dead in his tracks.

"Throw down your gun and come into camp, jasper!" the loud voice of Keller burst on his ears. "I've got you dead to rights this time."

Happy's eyes flew to the corner of the house. Hugging the side was Keller, a rifle resting across the projecting butt of a log. Happy made no move. The rifle spoke. The bullet licked up a furrow of dust at his feet and went whining on across the flat. Knowing from what he already had seen of Keller that the fellow would not hesitate to kill him without a fighting chance, he raised his hands slowly above his head and went forward.

"Hello, Keller!" he said coolly. "I didn't figure on putting back in here at your spread after my quick getaway last night. . . . I got my trails tangled up somehow."

"Where have you got your gun stashed?" Keller demanded, eyeing him venomously along the rifle barrel.

"Cleaned slicker than a skinned rabbit," Happy said.

"Don't try any of that funny business on me. No hog-leg? Yank that forty-five of yours and toss it down. . . . Just plenty quick."

"Had to throw it away along with my chaps and cartridge belt back yonder when I fell into the river." Happy shot back. "But I've got the whole layout charged up to you, Keller, along with that crack saddle horse of mine you killed."

"You'll always have them coming," the inspector snarled, wincing with pain as he moved the bandaged arm Happy had wounded at the river bluffs the night before. "That silver mounted saddle you stole from me would pay for all the lousy trappings you'll ever own. And my horse—what became of it? And drilling me last night—you'll pay for it all, jasper. It's in the cards against you. You're just the gent I'm looking for. Showing up this way saves me a heap of trouble running you down, although I was in hopes you'd stayed in the river. Now that you've been fool enough to come back, you're under arrest. This time for keeps. There's just plenty of things I'm going to find out from you."

"Me too!" Happy threw back coldly. "And one of them is why you were holding Goldie Burton prisoner!"

"Holding who?" Keller demanded obviously puzzled.

"Goldie Burton! The girl I was helping to escape from here last night when you trailed us to the bluffs and I fell in the river. The poor kid jumped in after me. And I reckon—"

"What become of her?" Keller asked quickly. "Was she drowned?" His tone was both eager and anxious.

Praying that he was wrong, yet fearful that he was not, it was on the tip of Happy's tongue to answer affirmatively. Instead he evaded the question.

"I haven't been able to locate her," he said. "A flood caught us in midstream."

"That's too bad," the inspector said with mock sincerity. "Too damned bad, because she was such a handsome little filly."

The look of joy that crossed his face made Happy boil. "Who is she and why were you holding her prisoner?" he demanded hotly.

"Who's who?" Keller asked with maddening innocence.

"Goldie Burton, the girl who jumped into the river after me."

"You're a fine walloper to go around playing hero to every filly you meet!" sneered Keller.

"You swallow all they tell you and try to save them from some crazy deal they've trumped up when you don't even know their name!" He burst into laughter.

Happy bit back a hot remark. While Keller's sneering remarks set him to boiling with rage, they but voiced the doubts running through his own mind. He knew the girl had been a fortune-teller. Now it seemed that she was an adventuress as well; an adventuress whose real name he did not even know. Blazing anger took possession of him. Not so much toward Keller, although his impulse was to smash the leering face, but toward himself for heeding the pleas of the girl and following her blindly even after she had refused point blank to tell him anything of herself. He wondered what Keller knew of her; what alias she was traveling under on the river.

"I don't see why the death of any girl, no matter who she is, should be so funny," he found himself saying frozenly.

"Who said I was tickled 'cause she was dead?" Keller growled, making a threatening gesture with the rifle. "I was laughing at you—the way she took you in. But that's enough of this kind of talk, jasper. I've got other things to settle with you—specially you shooting me in the arm back at the bluff and beating me up when I wasn't feeling good."

"Shooting you just evens us up," Happy

flashed. "You shot me. Only I gave you a chance and you didn't me. As far as you not feeling good when I busted you, I notice you felt good enough to try and hold that thirsty herd of Rocking Chairs off of water. And you lied about how far it was to the river." He stepped forward until the muzzle of the rifle was almost touching him. "I don't get your game, Keller. . . . But I'm going to . . . You're going to think all hell has busted loose if it isn't dead on the level."

"That's plenty of your lip!" Keller rasped out, backing away to whip out his Colt with his uninjured hand and rest the rifle upright against the log house. "You've shot off your head all you're going to. Get into the house there now or I'll drill you. And be damned sure you keep your hands touching sky!"

CHAPTER XX

With no alternative, Happy did as he was bid. He rounded the corner of the house to enter through the same door to which he had staggered after the storm. Again inside the dining room his gaze whipped about. He recalled in startling detail everything that had occurred in that room the night before and which, in the rush of subsequent events, seemed ages ago. He backed against the wall suddenly conscious of a haunting sensation that had been with him for hours, yet which until now he had been unable to fathom. But in this room he seemed to feel the presence of the girl and, though it rankled, he was forced to admit that adventuress though she might be he could not drive her from his mind.

"What's all this horse play about?" he demanded of Keller, who had halted just within to look around nervously. "I'm getting damned sick of it. All you seem to be able to think of is scrapping with me or trying to arrest me. You've made more hell for me in the least time than any walloper I ever stacked up against. I want to know what your game is—and I want to know damned fast."

"We're not playing any game," Keller snarled. "You're just under arrest, that's all."

"But a man has got a right to know what he is being arrested for!" Happy flashed. "Where's your warrant?"

"Never mind the warrant! You don't need warrants for rustlers on Powder River."

"When did I rustle?"

"I'm not the judge! You pump him. I'm the jasper who is going to put you behind bars."

Realizing that he would get no satisfaction from the fellow, who, now, he was half inclined to believe, was persecuting him solely out of revenge, Happy ceased his questioning abruptly.

"Any law on Powder River against giving me a drink of water and a bite to eat?" he demanded.

"Don't know what the law is, but I'm telling you to go without as far as I'm concerned," Keller flung back. "After I get you where you won't make another break I'll give you grub and water—if I feel like it." His beady eyes snapped to a door at the far end of the room, beyond the shattered window pane through which Goldie and Happy had crawled. Sight of that pane, he himself had broken, again loosed in Happy a flood of disturbing thoughts.

"Get through that door there!" Keller ordered abruptly.

Happy ignored the command for a moment, cast about for some way to throw the fellow off his guard and wrest the forty-five from him. But no avenue of escape appearing to his fagged brain, he could only obey. He turned slowly and, without a word, did as he was bid.

"Now up those stairs!" Keller snarled when they had come into a dimly-lighted hallway. "Open the first door at the top. I'm just a step behind, snorting to shoot—bat an eye and I'll drop you!"

Another quick survey that offered no hope for turning the tables and Happy wearily climbed the flight of creaking stairs, decidedly uncomfortable in the knowledge of the forty-five bearing down between his shoulder blades. At the first door he stopped as he was ordered. The knob yielded to his touch. He stepped inside a room so filled with boxes he was barely able to move. Before he could turn to voice the question that sprang to his lips, the door banged behind him. A key grated in the lock. He heard Keller's heavy tread moving downstairs. The inspector was chuckling to himself.

Taking violent hold on the anger that possessed him, Happy dropped onto the nearest box. When his eyes had become accustomed to the semi-darkness, he took stock of his surroundings. Boxes were piled to the ceiling; boxes were banked in tiers against the one window, through which only a meager light managed to creep.

Wondering, he got to his feet, hefted one. The boxes were filled with canned goods. The enormity of the supply amazed him. Then, as he thought the thing over, it was not so strange. The base of supplies obviously was far distant on Powder River; the cowtrails that served as roads probably impassable save during the summer months.

Lifting several of them down, he made himself a bed and stretched out full-length, the room itself no more gloomy than his thoughts. It seemed that for all his former confidence and assurance he suddenly had become pitifully impotent to cope with any situation. For the life of him he could not figure the thing out. While he was positive that Keller's actions were inspired by revenge, the charge of rustling—if indeed there was such a charge—would have to be based on the strays that had stampeded into the herd. He recalled Mournful's statement that they would not be found. He fell to hoping that the *segundo* had found the opportunity to work the tangled herd and throw the strange brutes back. The more he thought of the whole affair the more he began to lean toward Mournful's hunch immediately after the stampede—that the thing was a frame-up. But how it could be, or for what purpose, was beyond his comprehension.

Utter weariness finally forced him to abandon any attempt at trying to solve the riddle. Hard as was his improvised bed it offered a place to rest without the discomfort of the cold and heat, that he had endured for endless hours. For all the gnawing hunger and burning thirst that tormented him he fell into a fitful sleep.

But it was the pangs of hunger that awakened him. He straightened up cautiously, half expecting to hear the angry roar of Powder River and find himself surrounded by swirling, twisting water. But he caught hold of himself quickly and got his bearings. Aware, by the lowering light, that it was almost evening, once his mind had cleared he set about trying to evolve some plan of escape. To reach the window was out of the question. Keller would hear him moving the boxes. The door—he could smash it easily enough, but that would only draw the fire of the inspector. He cudgeled his aching brain. At the moment there seemed no way out of his dilemma. But eat and drink he must before the gnawing pains drove him to desperation.

"You poor fool!" he exclaimed, suddenly leaping up to peer at the labels on the ends of the boxes. "Laying in a grocery store and so hungry your belly thinks your throat's cut!" He pried off the lid of one of the boxes labeled: "Salmon." Then he continued his search until he located tomatoes. Presently he had a feast of canned goods piled about him. Seating himself, he opened them with his jack-knife, drank a can of tomatoes, which quickly assuaged his thirst, then fell greedily to his first meal in hours.

"Thanks, Mister Keller," he chuckled, feeling

almost gay when he had finished. "That was the best grub I ever ate. Fact is, I think right now I could bust you and take that gun away from you." Stretching out, he dozed comfortably, content with the world save for a tugging fear for Goldie which persisted in creeping into his mind.

"It's funny this outfit would have such a bunch of supplies?" he mused aloud. "Of course they're a long way from a railroad and there probably aren't many freighters in here. But who—" For no reason at all recurred to him Goldie's answer when he had asked her if Keller owned the Circle H.

"I don't know," the girl had said. "I'm trying to find out. When I do—" Then she had broken off to urge him to greater haste in escaping as they fled from the ranch-house.

"Wonder what she meant when she said she was trying to find out?" he pondered. "It's a cinch these canned goods are consigned to the owner of the spread. There must be a carload, or more of them. Might not be a bad idea to find out while I've got the chance."

He lay flat on his back idly trying to decipher the stenciled name on the lid of one of the boxes above him. "Roundup, Wyoming," stared back at him. He had heard of the place; a cowtown far back in the Powder brakes. The stuff had been freighted over long miles of treacherous trails. But, rising quickly he peered at the stenciled name of the consignee. That look became an incredulous stare.

"Ed Jackson!" The name struck him dumb with amazement. "Ed Jackson, Roundup, Wyoming," he repeated after a time. "Why he never had money enough in his life to buy all this stuff! Besides, Jackson's post-office is Halfway, Dakota. What in hell has Ed Jackson got to do with the Circle H?"

To his mind flashed a picture of the stranger who had crossed the yard to the corrals that morning as he had come in only to face the rifle in the hands of Keller—the stranger with the loose-hipped gait that had been so familiar. Instantly he knew. It had been Ed Jackson. Ed Jackson was the man who had loped away at the head of the Circle H punchers just as he had come up; and ten chances to one Ed Jackson was the mysterious stranger whom Goldie had said Keller's men had gone to meet after the storm!

His imprisonment, Keller's hatred and persecution were clear to him now. It was Ed Jackson's revenge. Jackson had ridden toward the river crossing in the direction the big Rocking Chair herd had taken. It could mean but one thing. . . . He knew all he wanted to of Ed Jackson.

Gone in a twinkling was his apathy. It was the Happy Day of the Rocking Chair; confident, courageous, his eyes flecked with pin-points of flame. Leaping to the door he kicked it. He waited, listening breathlessly. But if Keller remained in the house he raised no protest.

Happy kicked again. Still no challenge. Seizing up a case of canned goods, he hurled it against the panels, splintering them. He squeezed through into the hallway, dark now in the waning light of evening and paused to listen. No sound but the thumping of his own heart broke the gripping stillness. He stole on to the stairs. He was in the act of descending the first one when a forty-five cracked from below. The bullet went screaming past him to bury itself in the ceiling above him. He leaped back into the gloom waiting for his unseen assailant, whom he knew to be Keller, to press the attack.

Seconds passed with nerve-racking slowness. But the shot was not repeated. Chafing under the delay, cramped in his nerve-taut position, Happy shifted slightly. At the sound the Colt spoke again. The lead sang a song of hate past his ear. He dodged back, his mind working swiftly. From the direction in which the bullets had come he reasoned that Keller was at the bottom and to one side of the stairs. Returning stealthily to the room he secured a box of the canned goods. Stealing to the top of the stairs, he shoved it out in plain sight. In the semi-darkness, Keller mistook his target. Six jets of flame stabbed the gloom!

When the last deafening reverberation had

crashed down upon him, Happy lifted the box, which was dripping with juice from the punctured cans inside, raised it above his head to send it hurtling below. A howl of pain, followed by a sputtering curse arose. In three mighty bounds he was down the stairs. Before Keller could stagger to his feet from among the burst cans, Happy was upon him. But where the other encounters with the fellow had been easy, this one was a different story. Wounded though he was, the inspector seized him before he could land a blow. The fight turned into a wrestling match; a game of which Happy knew little and at which he was almost powerless in the strong grip of Keller. Up and down the hallway they rolled, Happy taxing his muscles to the limit, Keller apparently able to reserve some of his prodigious strength.

In a few minutes the strain began to tell on Happy. For all his food and rest the grueling experiences of the preceding hours had undermined his strength. The mighty effort brought him to a realization of the punishment he had endured. He fought gamely. But Keller bore him backwards, climbed on top of him and was squeezing the breath from his body with a vise-like knee-grip, his fingers clawing for a throat hold.

Nearer and nearer came those fingers, groping like deadly tentacles in the dusk. Happy tried to bridge. Keller's weight was too great. He attempted to squirm from under the huge body. In this too he failed. He experienced something of the sensation of hopeless defeat he had known when the current sucked him away from the ford after Goldie had landed.

Sheer desperation in the knowledge that Keller would show no mercy lent him the strength to fight on. Yet he was swiftly near the point where he must give up. He now could see Keller's ugly face leering above him, one eye still half closed, his thick lips split.

Happy's flailing arms came in contact with one of the cans. His fingers closed about it. Putting all his strength into a last effort, he sent the can smashing into Keller's face.

The blow loosened the fellow's hold. Happy rolled him off and lurched to his feet. Keller too came up, bawling with fury, to whip out his gun.

"You damned bluffer!" Happy panted. "It's empty. Don't you suppose I've had sense enough to figure on that!"

With a snarl Keller bored in, attempting to use the butt of the Colt as a club. Happy managed to dodge. Then of a sudden he got the opening he sought. Again the two lightning punches that had sent Keller down before. They landed with sickening smacks. Keller crumpled to the floor.

Happy leaped across the prone figure and started for the door, only to hesitate an instant and turn back. Stooping quickly, he dragged off the inspector's boots. When he had pulled them onto his own feet he stripped off the fellow's chaps.

"I always did admire silver conchas," he muttered. "But I never could afford them. . . . These here are beauts. Of course, the chaps are a little big and plenty sticky with tomato juice; but I reckon they'll pretty up nice. Told you I had an outfit charged against you, Keller. This one will just about pay for the duds I had to leave in the river."

Slipping into the chaps, he jerked them to the last notch. Groping about in the dark he found Keller's hat and forty-five. Buckling the inspector's cartridge belt around him and ramming the empty Colt into its holster, he made for the door.

CHAPTER XXI

In a half dozen swift strides Happy Day had crossed the dining room of the Circle H ranch-house and was outside in the light of early evening. Secure in the belief that if there had been anyone around they would have come to investigate the shots and the noise of the fight, he ran awkwardly across the yard. A quick survey of the horse pasture showed the cavvy ponies still grazing nearby. He started for the barn—he would find a saddle and—

Suddenly he recalled the brute he had seen Keller leave inside the round corral as he approached. It was saddled. If it could be forced to travel at all it would save the time of locating a saddle and catching up a cavvy horse. He dropped the poles, strode into the corral. The horse snorted and lunged back on the hackamore rope with which it was tied. Unfastening it quickly, Happy half dragged the brute from the enclosure. It danced around angrily as he tried to mount. Checking it, he swung up. Once settled in the saddle, he let it go. With a bawl of rage it dropped its head and pitched toward the outer gate.

The next few minutes found the world spinning for Happy. But he had been there before. He raked the brute from withers to rump with Keller's big-roweled spurs. It was going high into the air, sun-fishing as it came down, landing first in front then behind like a stone-crusher. Twice he started for leather. Both times pride held him back and with a gigantic effort he regained his slipping knee-grip.

Of a sudden he found the end of a lariat looped over the horn. Riding recklessly until he was able to unloosen it, he started working on the brute. With the first blow it bolted straight for the gate that Jackson and his men had left down that morning. Once outside, it pivoted on its hind legs, let forth a hoarse bawl and headed at a mad run along a cowtrail in the direction of the river.

It quickly ran itself into a lather. But Happy made no attempt to check its wild flight. Behind was Keller, who might come to at any moment, quickly catch up the swiftest of the cavvy ponies in the horse pasture and give pursuit. Ahead somewhere was Ed Jackson and the Circle H men, whom he had no desire to meet—at least until he had overtaken his herd. His one hope seemed to lie in forging along at the best pace the green outlaw could maintain. He kept his eyes glued on the wide gap in the river bluffs, praying fervently that he had not been mistaken; that the spot was the ford where Mournful had crossed with the Rocking Chairs.

Then he could hear the river. But now the crash

and boom had been displaced by a swishing little louder than that created by the wind rushing past his ears. Along a well-worn trail that ran into the gap raced the horse. The water burst into view. Happy's heart leaped with joy. They had struck the river at the ford. There were no bluffs ahead. The trail ran gradually to the water's edge!

Without slackening speed the outlaw plunged into the river, cleaving the water with its chest and filling Happy's face with spray. Then it was swimming for dear life, Happy, feet out of the stirrups and drawn up beneath him, aboard and dripping.

Reaching the opposite bank without mishap, the animal lurched out of the water. But the swim by no means had wasted its strength. In spite of the heaving breath, that rasped croupily in its throat and tore at its lungs, it was gone again at a mad pace along a cowtrail that ran on to a table and sloped gently to the badlands, which, in turn, stretched away to the verge of sight.

But the brute could not maintain the killing gait. It began to tire. Happy's rowels goaded it on until it was merely crow-hopping, off balance. Presently the spurs had no effect. The outlaw ignored the slicing pain, slowed down. Its best tricks spent without having unseated its rider, it became docile. Like an old cow pony it loped across the flats now drenched with a purple haze in the twilight.

With the Circle H far behind and little to concern him save a chance meeting with Jackson and his punchers, Happy fell to thinking back over the incidences that had occurred with such startling suddenness since his arrival in the badlands. As the green bronc loped along stiff-legged, the harrowing events of the swift-moving drama became as a hazy dream; the girl but a wraith that would ever linger in his memory. It all lay behind him now. Ahead was his herd, apparently safe, somewhere south of Powder River. A sense of complete satisfaction settled over him, undisturbed except for the knowledge that Ed Jackson also was somewhere ahead. For what purpose he did not know.

Night fell. On and on he went, locked in thought that took no notice of the miles. The darkness thickened until the badlands were completely shrouded in a mantle of black. Then the moon came swimming up, a great yellow ball in a sea of gold, flooding the flats with a soft pale light that transformed the brush and buttes to eerie, misshapen monsters. Higher and higher into the star-lit sky it made its lazy way. Farther and farther south rode Happy, so tired now he could scarcely hold open his eyes, jerking himself out of dozes from time to time to peer about.

Yet not until long after the moon had crossed the zenith and the flats had begun to grow dim in its waning light did he sight a sign of life—a distant campfire. Hoping that at last he had overtaken the Rocking Chair herd, he roweled the weary pony into a lope. As they came nearer to the fire the animal, snorting in terror at sight of the flames lapping into the motionless air, attempted to bolt. But Happy held it to a straight course.

He pulled up presently trying to locate the mess-wagon. He could not find it. Neither could he spot any bed-rolls scattered about the fire. A vague uneasiness assailed him. Berating himself for the suspicious nature he had so suddenly acquired, he roweled the snorting pony to the edge of the circle of light cast by the fire. There it stopped trembling, a terrified gleam in its eyes. Still he could see no one, although his quick ear caught the restless movement of cattle on bed-ground some distance below.

He opened his mouth to shout. A gruff voice, that set his frayed nerves to strumming, came out of the gloom on the opposite side of the fire.

"Where in hell have you been all this time, Keller?"

That voice belonged to Ed Jackson!

Happy went rigid in his saddle, his mind lightning fast. Obviously Jackson was expecting Keller. Garbed as he was in the inspector's outfit, it was evident that the glimpse Jackson had of the flashing conchas in the firelight had deceived him.

Happy resolved upon a desperate expediency to find out, if he could, why the erstwhile foreman of the Rocking Chair, and apparently the owner of the Circle H, was camped in the badlands without bed-rolls or wagon.

"I'm getting sick and tired of your stalling!" Jackson growled testily, before Happy was forced to reply. "Here I've been waiting half the night for you. Now, damn you, get busy!"

He strode angrily around the campfire toward Happy. But the bronc snorted and shied away violently.

"And you rode that damned outlaw!" Jackson snarled, halting. "Of all the broke cavvy stuff in that home pasture you were too damned lazy to catch yourself a horse and rode that outlaw just to be smart—and after me warning you not to. Hereafter you're going to do as I tell you, Keller, or I'm going to bust that mullet head of yours wide open. Get out there on herd duty where you belong. And if that bronc scares the critters I'll kill you. We're holding every hoof we can gather right below. One of the boys is way down yonder ready to touch off the fireworks with the crack of dawn!"

Thankful that he had not been compelled to give himself away by speaking, Happy rode toward where he could hear the herd. That Jackson was up to some devilment he was positive. What it was he could not for the life of him figure out.

Nor had the fellow's words given him the faintest clew. However, now that he was into the thing he resolved grimly to go on night herd and keep his eyes and ears open.

But his plans miscarried. No sooner had he reached the herd than the bronc, for no reason he could figure out, downed its head and with a terrified snort started pitching. Straight among the bedded cattle it went, bawling like a frightened calf. Taken completely off his guard, Happy fought desperately for a time to retain his seat. Above the pounding hoofs, he heard the other punchers galloping up. Then Jackson's voice.

"I told you to catch up a broke string horse and not to ride that damned bronc." Jackson was cursing out of the sudden darkness as the moon scudded behind a bank of clouds in its downward flight. "I'll kill you if it's the last thing I ever do. Run that outlaw out of there before the critters go like a bat out of hell!"

But Happy had no time to heed him. If the outlaw had pitched hard when first he had mounted it back at the Circle H, tired as it now was, it was doing the job twice as well. In and out along the edge of the herd it seesawed, lunging wildly into the air, landing on one leg at a time like a waltzing horse, its body bent like a hairpin, its whistling nostrils buried between its fetlocks.

Shadowed forms were bounding up on every side. Frantic bawls thundered out of the gloom.

With every passing moment Happy expected to hear the herd stampede. But he was powerless to prevent it. It required all of his skill and strength to stay with the plunging brute, that was kinking his neck and twisting his spine each time it came down with an impact that knocked a groan from its own body.

Then Jackson was beside him, trying desperately to haze him from among the cattle, cursing at the top of his voice. They were on the edge of the herd. The outlaw paused for a second in its wild gyrations to blow.

"What the hell is going on here?" a booming voice demanded.

Happy's heart sank. There was no mistaking that voice. It was Keller!

The squeak of leather told him Jackson had whirled in his saddle.

"Keller," Jackson roared. "I thought—" he stopped blankly. "Isn't this you? Who the hell is it on this bronc?"

Happy felt rather than saw blazing eyes boring suspiciously into his. He fingered his Colt, waiting for the showdown that was bound to come.

"He stole my chaps," Keller cried miserably. "And my gun and that bronc—and busted me when I'm hurt. I come on a cavvy horse. It's that Happy Day, a cowhand for—"

"Happy Day!" Jackson bawled. "Happy Day is

the boss of the Rocking Chair herd. The jasper I . . ." He broke off. "Kill the . . . ! Kill him. He is the one I told you to . . . Keller, I'll beat you to death for this if it's the last thing I ever do!" A jet of flame stabbed the darkness which was deepening as the moon sank farther behind the solid mass of clouds on the horizon. A bullet clipped Keller's hat from Happy's head.

"I'm not to blame, Jackson!" Keller was bellowing. "That owl-faced Rocking Chair jasper told me Jack Halliday was the boss—after that I got to thinking you said Jack Halliday. I—"

The rest of his words were lost to Happy in a sudden rush of air as the terrified outlaw again downed its head and pitched back into the herd. Lead whistled harmlessly past him. Hammering up and down in the gloom, he was an impossible target except for a chance bullet. He fought desperately to turn back and have it out with Jackson and Keller. But he could not. The bronc was unmanageable, its rope-burned, bleeding nose numb to the frantic sawing on the hackamore. Straight through the herd it went, sending cattle lunging away in terror.

CHAPTER XXII

But the shots "pinging" out of the darkness, the furious shouts, the madly-pitching outlaw had done their work. Pandemonium broke loose. Jackson's bellows were drowned in a bedlam of bawls. The herd quit the bedground in wild stampede. Even the green bronc seemed to sense the terror of the moment. Shaking with fright, it ceased its pitching to whirl like a top, kicking viciously at the running brutes that came too near for safety.

The thing was over as quickly as it had begun. Caught far back in the herd, the cattle soon poured past Happy. Safe from the thundering hoofs, he dragged the pony about, and started over to where he had left Jackson. But the fellow's voice drifted back from far below.

". . . is Happy Day, I'm trying to tell you!" snatches of Jackson's furious yells at Keller came back to Happy. "I'll kill you for this you mullet-headed . . ."

Came Keller's roar. "You didn't say Happy Day, you—you said Halliday. How was I to know? I—"

Presently the angry voices were drowned in the roar of clicking horns and pounding hoofs that came out of the night like the steady hum of a great planing mill.

For several seconds Happy sat motionless, stroking his nervous pony's neck and staring into the darkness. "I don't know whether to bust you or hug you, horse," he muttered. "It isn't right to stampede cows even if they are Jackson's. But if it hadn't been for your pitching and the moon covering up just when it did they'd have plugged me—nothing surer than that.

"By God!" he exclaimed. "I haven't got a living soul to thank that I haven't been killed but Mournful. He's the walloper who told Keller my name was Happy Day; that Jack Halliday had gone up the trail the first time we met up with that inspector. I figured he was just lying then. But he must of known what he was doing!"

He paused again to listen to the stampede, the noise of which was swiftly dying to a rumble in the distance. Suddenly he jerked on the hackamore rope.

"The Rocking Chair herd is somewhere below!" he blurted aloud. "Those critters must be heading direct for them!" He lifted his startled horse with the rowels. It lunged away, too frightened now to pitch.

Louder and louder grew the hum ahead, as Happy's spurs goaded the horse to its mightiest effort. Stark terror lent it speed. The wind whistled through Happy's flying hair, stung his eyes.

"We've got to lead that herd, horse!" he kept

mumbling. “If the Rocking Chairs are ahead . . .”

Outlaw that it was the pony seemed to understand. It was running steadily, desperately, its head on a level with its tail, its hoofs beating a tattoo on the parched gumbo. Clumps of brush and dry washes were taken in low-flying leaps which sent the lather from its foam-flecked neck back into Happy’s face.

Then, directly ahead in the darkness, loomed the lags of the stampede. Instinctively the horse pulled aside to flash by them. Alongside the lumbering herd it raced, its breath rasping in its throat, its flanks heaving. Dimly-outlined, cursing punchers flew past. Then Jackson’s furious bawls and Keller’s thunderous shouts beat above the tumult on Happy’s ears.

“That’s a fine team of coyotes to be teamed up!” Happy mused grimly. “Wonder what they’re up to . . . What they were holding that big bunch of critters back there for?”

But he had no time to think. With a mighty effort the pony drew even with the leaders; thundered past. Then they were ahead and to one side of the stampede. But this new killing effort was beginning to tell on the green bronc. Yet Happy dared not slacken speed until he was certain the Rocking Chair herd was out of the path of the stampede.

Oftener now was he forced to gouge the pony with the rowels. Each prick sent it lunging on in a burst of speed. But its croupy breath told him plainer than words that it had broken its wind; that its first effort as a saddle pony also would be its last!

With fearful expectancy he watched ahead. Then far, far away he caught the twinkle of a campfire.

"It's them, horse," he muttered. "If we can make it I'll buy you and you'll never have a saddle on you again to your dying day."

He stroked the pony's neck. It responded gamely to the caress. But no longer was it running evenly. Body bowed, head to one side told of hopeless, heart-breaking effort.

"Hang on, horse, hang on!" Happy encouraged desperately. "Another mile and we'll win!"

In spite of the pony's mighty attempt the thunder of the hoofs behind was increasing in volume. Ahead Happy could see shadowed forms of men darting back and forth across the fire. A horse galloped away, flashed past him. Another!

"Good old Mournful!" Happy cried. "He's already caught on. Got up the cavvy. He knows it doesn't thunder like this on a moonlit night!"

With a terrific burst of speed, the pony cleared a dry wash, stumbled and went down to bump along on its knees. Happy jerked on the hackamore rope. But it could not right itself. He quit it in a flying leap. The brute quivered, snorted and straightened out.

"Mournful!" he shouted, running toward the fire. "A stampede's coming!"

"Happy!" His name was a glad cry on the lips of the *segundo*, who spurred forward to meet him. "We heard it. All the boys I can spare are out to meet it. The rest of them are guarding our stuff. Climb aboard your nag! The herd needs us."

Happy ran back to the pony's side. It had not moved.

"It's—" he said grimly. "The gamest little nag I ever forked."

"Throw a leg across the night horse!" Mournful shouted. "There at the wagon! Hustle!"

Happy tore past the fire in the direction of the mess-wagon. A mounted figure he had not noticed before was framed for an instant in the light.

"Goldie!" he cried, stopping dead in his tracks.

"Happy!" her joyous tone thrilled him. Before he knew what he was about he had rushed to the side of her horse and seized her hand. The grasp she gave him set the blood hammering in his temples. "Hurry, Happy!" she urged in a tremulous voice.

He jerked loose the bridle reins of the night horse and swung up, his mind in a turmoil. Sight of the girl had loosed a flood of strange emotions that overwhelmed him. Adventuress though she might be he suddenly knew deep in his heart that he loved her! He wheeled his mount. Mournful already had disappeared. Goldie was waiting.

"This way!" she cried.

Together they bolted into the night toward the Rocking Chair herd.

They quickly overtook Mournful. But before a word could be spoken the staccato bark of several forty-fives rolled across the badlands.

"What's that?" Happy demanded, whirling in his saddle to stare back into the darkness.

"Just the Rocking Chair boys busting up that stampede," Mournful said sourly. "I told them to stop it if they had to kill every running critter." He peered ahead at the shadowy forms of their own cattle getting lazily to their feet. "But tell me something about yourself. How . . . Where . . ."

Another volley cut him short. "Reckon they're knocking them off right smart," he observed. "You didn't get to see what critters they were, did you? Wonder what riled them up?"

"I did," Happy admitted. "I was forking a game little bronc I—borrowed from Keller. It pitched among them!"

"Haven't we had enough herd mixing without you causing more?" Mournful growled. "Every time we've turned around since you left there has been a bunch of strays stampeding into our stuff."

"You've been cutting them out, haven't you?" Happy asked anxiously.

"Cutting them out?" Mournful snorted. "They've been coming so fast all the hands on Powder River couldn't cut them out. What did you say that stampeding bunch was branded?"

"Circle H's," Happy replied, staring through the darkness at the silent girl. With an effort he stifled a longing to question her concerning her escape and how she had managed to find the Rocking Chair camp—and Mournful. Yet it seemed so sadly out of place in view of the weightier matters at hand.

"You said back yonder at the ranch you'd find out sometime who was the boss of that spread?" he asked her. "Do you know yet?"

"No!" It was Mournful who answered, a new note of interest in his usually sad tone. "Do you?"

"Ed Jackson!"

Mournful jerked his horse to its haunches. "I had a . . ." he began. "How'd you find out, Happy?"

Quickly Happy told of the discovery he had made while a prisoner in the storage room at the Circle H.

"That's it!" blurted out Mournful to the girl. "I told you."

"Told her what?" demanded Happy.

Another volley crashing on the night air, checked Mournful's reply.

"All that shooting isn't to stop a stampede!" the

segundo remarked. "It sounds like a gun fight to me. You didn't see anybody with those critters, did you, Happy?"

"Jackson and Keller—"

"Ed—Jackson—on—Powder!" Mournful dragged his horse around in the trail. "You two stay with our stuff!" he ordered sharply. "I'll—" He stopped to sniff the air. "Happy!" he cried. "Smell! Smoke!"

Happy's eyes flew to the east. The first flush of dawn was slowly spreading over the sky. Came to him in a flash what Jackson had said when he had mistaken him for Keller back at the Circle H campfire.

"There is a man way down yonder ready to start the fireworks at the crack of dawn!" had been the fellow's words.

"Prairie fire!" he cried. "Jackson's man started it. He told me so, thinking I was Keller. We're in a nice jackpot now."

"Get the boys to circling our herd!" Mournful lashed out. "Start them back up the trail."

"But they'll meet that other herd," Happy protested.

"They might just as well," Mournful flared, with an amazing display of spirit. "They're only about half Rocking Chairs now anyway. And things are going to happen around here pronto." With that he was gone.

Happy turned to the girl. "You'd better go back

to camp and wait till we get the stuff to moving," he said solicitously. "You—"

"The idea of you talking to me like this after what we've been through together!" she retorted angrily. "I can trail a herd with the best man you've got in your crew. Come on!"

She galloped past him. He followed. Warning his men, who were delighted to find he was safe, they circled the herd together. In a short time they had the stretching brutes in motion on the back trail. He peered ahead anxiously. But apparently Mournful and the Rocking Chair boys had been successful in stopping the stampede for the thunderous roar of hoofs and the crack of Colts had ceased.

By now the streamers of color were creeping into the sky. When he could see, Happy looked back. Here and there fluffy clouds were drifting over the rim of the badlands. Not a breath of air stirred. The pungent odor of smoke increased with each passing moment. A calm as dead as that preceding a terrific storm lay on the flats.

The sun came up, a blood-red ball in a leaden sky. A finger of flame reached over the horizon to drag down the tufts of grass and burned in puffs of fleecy white.

Riding sidewise in his saddle, Happy tried desperately to get the thing straight in his mind. But he failed utterly. Somewhere behind it all he could see Jackson's scheming. But why had

Jackson had his men start the fire? What did he hope to gain by it?

From Jackson his thoughts flew to Keller who, without doubt, would have killed him at the outset had it not been for Mournful's lie about Jack Halliday. The more he pondered the mix-up the more muddled he became. Of only one thing he was certain. By stampeding the Circle H herd—Jackson himself had admitted that it was every hoof the spread could gather—in some way he had upset the plans of the erstwhile foreman of the Rocking Chair!

He gave up the puzzle presently to look back. The southern horizon was a mass of swaying, shifting colors. The flames were creeping forward steadily, rolling white smoke high into the overcast sky. From below came small bunches of cattle, running before the fire and increasing the uneasiness of the Rocking Chair critters, which stopped from time to time to sniff the air fearfully. With each whiff of smoke, the herd went forward a little faster until the whole column was moving at a lumbering trot.

CHAPTER XXIII

Shouting for one of the men to lend a hand to the lagging cook, Happy watched anxiously until the team had been hooked up, the bed-rolls loaded and the mess-wagon started back along the trail.

When his few riders had flanked the herd, he turned to the quiet girl. She met his gaze shyly.

"I've got to point them, Goldie," he said. "You stay here where—"

"Where there isn't any danger," she flashed. "Not on your life, Happy Day. I'm riding the point with you."

"But it's a case of holding them back now. That isn't the cinch just pointing them is," protested.

Her only answer was to rowel up beside him as he went forward to the head of the herd, a position fraught with danger.

Big, raw-boned steers, their eyeballs showing white, now were breaking constantly. The cursing, shouting punchers fought savagely to hold them in line. Between anxious looks ahead and behind, Happy found time for an occasional surreptitious glance at the girl. Her utter lack of fear, her easy grace in the saddle, the manner in which she went about holding the nervous herd was evidence that she was no stranger to cowland. It puzzled him deeply, how she, a fortune-teller, an adventuress . . .

He clicked his teeth grimly on the thoughts that came tumbling into his mind. No matter what she was, what she had done, she had proved herself a heroine to him.

He tried to think of something to say to her. But he suddenly had become speechless, conscious of a thousand questions he could ask but unable to voice a single one of them. He seemed capable of nothing in her presence except to stare at her rudely when she turned to look up or down the trail, her golden hair caressing her cheeks, the rosy tint of health playing in her face, her slender body swinging gracefully to the motion of her horse.

He tore his gaze away from the picture she made to glance at the cattle, which were lumbering along, noses to the ground, mouths open, slaver flecking their sagging jowls, bawls of terror rumbling in their throats.

The sun crawled higher. The heat became sickening. Sweat rolled from man and beast. Happy lifted his hat to brush matted hair away from his forehead.

"Will we make it to the river?" he asked, to cover his embarrassed silence.

"We usually do get out of tight places," she flashed. "Rapids, for instance. I'm dying to know how you came through after you saved me at the risk of your own life."

He started to reply. But he had no time. For

at that moment they topped a hogback. Directly ahead, across a ravine, loomed the Circle H herd, milling wildly. Between the brutes and the Rocking Chairs, Mournful and his punchers lolled in their saddles. Scattered about were a score or more of dead cattle.

"Reckon there is the merry hell to pay now," Happy said. "Killing those critters is going hard with us."

A threatening roar brought him whirling about, rigid in his stirrups. The gaunt Rocking Chair leaders had topped the rise to stop short and throw up their heads belligerently. He dug the spurs into his mount. It lunged over beside the girl just as a great bellow ascended from the herd.

He barely had time to slap her mount across the rump and send it leaping to safety when the Rocking Chair herd broke into a run, heads down, bawling defiantly.

The next few minutes were a nightmare of noise, dust, confusion. Across the draw the Rocking Chairs thundered. They met the Circle H's head on. The scene the day they had arrived above the river was reenacted. . . . Cattle with locked horns, rigid, pushing, grunting . . . Bawls, snorts, roars, rising in a tumult to roll deafeningly across the flats. Dust, heat, and now the acrid odor of smoke . . . Flames lapping behind . . . A restless, heaving sea of rumps ahead.

Happy looked around for the girl. She was beside him.

Suddenly from out of the churning mass roweled two cursing horsemen. A forty-five cracked. One of the two threw up his arms, pitched headlong to the ground.

Then the other was riding directly toward Happy, blue smoke from his hot-barreled Colt writhing about his head. Goldie screamed. Mournful almost threw his horse off its feet as he whirled, came plunging back to drag it to its haunches.

"Come on, Jackson." Happy lashed out frozenly. "It's a showdown now—you or me—"

A moment without breath or motion. Then . . . Two shots cracked as one. Some of the cattle paused in their fighting to stare inquisitively.

Ed Jackson swayed in his saddle, clutched wildly for the horn, missed, pitched headlong to the ground.

"Happy!" the girl cried. "You're hurt."

"Hurt, hell," Happy muttered. "I'm—I'm . . ." His voice trailed off. He lurched against the horn. Mournful and Goldie caught him as he let go, lowered him to the ground.

Happy stared up at them with glassy eyes. "Goldie—" His words were thick, barely audible. "Goldie, nothing . . . I don't even know her name . . . Dark man . . . Was Ed Jackson . . . What does your occult power . . ."

His voice broke. He struggled valiantly against the mantle of darkness closing in upon him. Then everything faded.

Above the infernal roar of the scalding blood in his temples Happy was vaguely conscious of voices far, far away. He strained to catch them.

"Well, I reckon that cleans the slate." He recognized Mournful's tone. Yet now it had dropped the whine; was strangely strong and forceful. "Ed Jackson didn't have a soul to blame but himself. I warned him back at Halfway he'd stop lead if he interfered with this herd."

"And I tried so hard to warn Happy," came the tiny sob-racked voice of a girl.

Hazy as were his impressions, Happy thrilled to the sound of that voice. Goldie's! He would recognize it anywhere. He had heard it on the threshold of eternity; it had come to him out of the black void of semi-consciousness. Adventuress she might be but no matter what her name, the overwhelming emotions that jerked him back to sensibility told him he loved her—loved her madly, unreasonably. Suddenly he knew he had loved her since that first meeting in Halfway.

"He figured you were just a carnival fortune-teller and took the whole thing as a joke," Mournful was saying. "Thank God, he isn't hurt too bad—just a clean flesh wound. There, it's all bandaged up pretty good. I doubt if it bothers him except for a little pain and stiffness—but that arm's pretty well shot up. That gash I took the bandage off of—looks like—"

"Don't you remember of me telling you about Keller shooting him when he staggered exhausted into the Circle H after the storm?" came Goldie's voice again. "I bandaged it—"

Keller! The name brought everything rushing back to Happy, cleared his brain. He raised up onto an elbow, stared around groggily. Mournful was directly above him, had just finished bandaging his arm, and his head was pillowed in Goldie's lap. She was brushing the hair back from his sweat-beaded forehead. Jerking away, he lurched to his feet, to stand swaying dizzily.

"Keller!" he rasped out. "Where is he?"

"Yonder." Mournful pointed to where the stock inspector sprawled lifeless on the ground, surrounded by Rocking Chair punchers. "Ed Jackson put him down—for keeps." He got to his feet to spring forward and seize hold of Happy as he started reeling away toward the group. "Sit down," he ordered sharply. "You need rest."

Happy sank to the ground, clutching his forearm, through which pains were shooting. "Keller, dead," he muttered dully. "And Jackson killed him. . . . He threatened to . . . Where is Jackson?"

"He stopped lead," Mournful announced solemnly. "Between the eyes."

"I hated to do it," Happy murmured.

"You didn't, kid," was the *segundo*'s amazing assertion. "I drilled Ed Jackson."

"But there were only two shots," Happy's brain was vividly clear although his muscles were in revolt.

Mournful passed over a forty-five.

"You must of gone hog-wild," he said reproachfully. "The gun you cracked down on Ed Jackson with was as empty as a hollow tooth."

Happy broke the cylinder to stare at the empty chambers. Then he remembered. In his haste to leave the Circle H after his last fight with Keller, he had seized up the empty Colt and made for the corral. In his excitement of riding the outlaw he had forgotten to refill it. He got slowly to his feet again, feeling better as the dizziness subsided.

"Thanks," he said huskily, extending his hand to Mournful. "That's the second time you've saved my life. Lying about my name back yonder the day we came to the river made Keller think Jack Halliday was boss of the herd instead of—"

"I don't know how you figure I lied," Mournful cut in, fixing him with that strange inscrutable glance.

"Keller had orders to drop . . . When you told him Jack Halliday . . ."

"Keller had orders to drop Jack Halliday," Mournful interrupted again. "I played him for the dumb kind that gets tangled in his own throw rope—Happy Day or Halliday; they both sounded alike to him. He didn't know that—"

"What?" Happy demanded.

"That Happy Day and Jack Halliday were the same. Climb down off your high horse, kid," Mournful snapped in a tone far different now from the nasal whine. "Goldie and I have known from the jump that you were young Jack Halliday; that you'd come down here to get the man who killed your father. You spilled it all when you were delirious back there in Halfway, after that gunplay with Jackson. The Old Man saw the resemblance the day he met you; and Ed Jackson saw it too. That's why he set out to get you."

Happy's gray eyes were upon him, but never by so much as a flicker did they betray the riotous emotions surging up in him.

"Was Jackson the dark man supposed to come into my life and raise twenty kinds of merry hell?" he asked quietly. "I'm not denying any longer that there is something in hunches."

"Ask her." Mournful jerked a thumb toward Goldie.

Happy turned on her questioningly. Her eyes fell before his steady gaze.

"Was Jackson the gent?" he repeated.

"No." She shot a glance over her shoulder toward Keller's body and shuddered. "There is the dark man."

"Keller?" Happy blurted out. "So you did know him when you warned me back at Halfway before I started up here!" Her obvious disclosure sent a new weight of doubt crashing down upon him. "He knew your name wasn't Goldie Burton, too . . . And you weren't a prisoner down at the Circle H?"

"I was a prisoner at the Circle H," she said coldly. "Simply because I would not explain to Keller why I was riding the trail alone after dark. I was only trying to find shelter from the storm. Keller never heard of Goldie Burton; they don't know me by that name on Powder River. I'd never seen Keller when I was in Halfway. But I knew about him; knew what he looked like; knew about this ranch up here. Taking you for a Rocking Chair man, who might come in here with the summer herd if Mr. Nathan sent one, I warned you of Keller—like I did all the rest of them."

Keller knew her by another name. She was a prisoner at the Circle H because she would not explain to Keller why she was riding the trail alone. The more she talked the more bewildered Happy grew.

He stood for a moment dividing his gaze between them, as though trying to link up their stories; figure out the connection between the two. It had been Mournful for whom she had pointed their herd; Mournful had danced attendance on her at Halfway. It had been Mournful for whom she had been willing to swim Powder River. Mournful! Mournful! The name drummed in his ears. Mournful seemed always to be first in her thoughts. For the moment he hated Mournful. But twice that same Mournful had saved his life. . . . Reason came swiftly to temper horrible jealousy, suspicion. He took violent hold of himself.

"I'm sorry I joshed you about her . . ." he found himself saying to the lanky puncher with the owlish face. "Whatever her name is, she's true blue; I'm mighty glad you found her again up here."

"What the devil are you talking about?" Mournful demanded. "What do you mean, glad I found her."

"Just what I said." Happy talked hurriedly, as though to rid himself of an unpleasant subject—a subject that not until the moment did he realize had tormented him for weeks. "I'm just glad you found her. And now . . . You two ought to team up."

The girl choked back a cry. The strangest laugh Happy had ever heard rumbled in Mournful's throat—a deep, throaty laugh, far unlike the whining Mournful he knew.

"What's so funny?" he asked. "The way you've gone around mooning since the fair at Halfway I figured you were stuck on her."

“Sure I am,” Mournful said, fastening him with that piercing glance. “She’s the finest girl I ever knew. But if it is all right with you, I’ll do my own proposing—when I get danged good and ready.” He stretched lazily. “Wonder how the prairie fire is coming on?”

CHAPTER XXIV

Mention of the fire sent Happy to running up the hogback. His blood-shot eyes swept toward the south. No longer were the flames clutching at the grass on the horizon. Only a faint smoke was visible. Evidently the fire had been checked. He turned as Mournful came up beside him.

"I took the guns away from those lousy Circle H jaspers and shagged them down there to beat out that fire they started." Mournful answered the question in his eyes. "A couple of our boys are riding herd on them with smoke-poles unlimbered and snorting to shoot. It looks like they got the best of it. We can be moving to water pronto. Sit down and rest, kid," he urged, taking Happy by the arm and leading him back to where the girl sat, idly tracing characters in the gumbo with a stick. "It doesn't seem much to be shot in the forearm; but the shock is plumb hell after all you've gone through."

"It isn't the wound that is bothering me," Happy said, throwing himself on the ground beside the girl. "It is all these doings I can't understand. Our herd is full of strays, you say? They've got to be worked out. Here I've been gone for hours—lost from the herd, scrapping with Keller. I'm a plumb failure as a trail boss; just like Ed Jackson bet I'd be. I locate the Rocking Chairs just in time to get into more trouble from this stampede. Then Jackson kills Keller and you kill Jackson. It's got things going 'round in my head."

"You've been through plenty to make things go around," Goldie said quietly. "Rest, please—for me."

Momentarily forgetful of his doubts, he flashed her a smile. "Thanks," he muttered, "but if I could get head or tail to the thing I'd feel a heap better."

"What, for instance?" Mournful inquired.

"The strays, you mentioned—the stampede the day we came to the river?"

"The minute I saw that herd I told you I had a hunch it was a frame-up, didn't I?" Mournful reminded.

"But do you think Keller knew they were in our herd?" demanded Happy.

"Think it!" Mournful snorted. "Say, the minute that gent lied about it being ten miles to the river I had his number. And he claimed he wasn't an inspector in here last spring. I'd never seen him, but I knew all I wanted to about him, and got his scheme pronto. He was too damned sure those strays were in there to suit me. The girl here saw those jaspers watching the herds mix!"

"Goldie?" Happy said incredulously. "That's why Keller was holding her a prisoner? That's why you told me to finish him off there after our first scrap? But why did you get me into that scrap with him?"

"I didn't figure he'd shoot your horse," Mournful answered. "Afterwards you busted into him so quick I couldn't stop you. Sure, that's why I told you to croak him. I knew who the gent was. The girl was stashed in a ravine taking in the whole works. She helped me point the herd across the river. And started back to where she lived. Dark caught her. After his scrap with you Keller nabbed her."

"Then the stampede was a frame-up just like you said?" Happy mused aloud. "But what for? What were those strays branded?"

"Circle H and Ringbone on the right hip!" Mournful answered. "Ours was Rocking Chair with Ringbone on the right hip."

"But you said nobody would ever find them."

"I said Keller would never find them," corrected Mournful. "Because I knew he wasn't looking for them."

"Wasn't looking for them?" in surprise.

"No. He knew they were in there packing their Circle H's. I saw right away that his scheme was to hold our herd until after dark, cut out a few head of Circle H's and a couple of hundred head of Rocking Chairs with a Ringbone on the right hip. It's so plumb simple now it doesn't seem like anything at all. They figured to get away with another thousand head of critters like they did last year. The brands on our stuff were fresh—two weeks old at the most and peeling; fly-time to boot—which means raw. If you ever stopped to figure it, a Rocking Chair only needs a half circle and a connecting line to be run into a Circle H. The Ringbone is just a road brand in Dakota. But it is a registered brand in Wyoming."

"So that was the game?" Happy exclaimed. "The Circle H holds two brands? Circle H and Ringbone on the right hip? Jackson paid Keller, who was a stock inspector? That gave him a right to stop a herd and work it for strays under the Wyoming law?"

"That's it. And they planted their own strays," Mournful growled. "But they fell down hard on this job."

"What do you mean?" demanded Happy quickly.

"The morning after I'd made that play before Keller about not having any strays in our herd, I tossed a rope onto a few of those critters and busted them. They were packing Circle H's all right. But one side of the Ringbone was crooked. You recklect that iron we had back at the ranch, with a bend in it, that we cussed so like the devil?"

"Yes!"

"Well, part of the Circle H's I threw were toting a Ringbone made with that crooked iron. And some of the connections in running the Rocking Chairs didn't fit?"

"Well, I'll be danged!" Happy blurted out, interested to the exclusion of everything else—even Goldie, who watched him with shyly admiring eyes. "It looks like we've got the goods on them all right. But how about the fire? I know Jackson's men touched it off but—"

"You upset their meathouse there," Mournful answered. "We—" he corrected himself quickly. "I—always figured Ed Jackson was behind the thing someway, but I couldn't get the lowdown on how. You're the one who did that, Happy. You found out he was the big squeeze at the Circle H. Ed never had enough to buy a ranch. He stole that thousand head he brought in here last spring from the Rocking Chair. That's how come the Circle H. And he figured he'd get another thousand in this herd. You nipped his game proper."

"I always thought he did," Happy grunted. "No wonder I couldn't spot any carcasses along the trail. But how did he figure to do it?"

"By stampeding Circle H's into our herd, cutting Rocking Chairs back and running the brands!" Mournful said. "But to do it they had to depend on Keller, the stock inspector. And you've been keeping Keller so busy scrapping with you he hasn't had time to work our herd, which is plumb lousy with Circle H's. Having given that big four-flusher orders to kill you on sight . . ."

"So that was the game?" Happy jerked out. "You were wise to that? That's why you claimed Jack Halliday had gone on up the trail that day. Was that why Goldie was so dead anxious to have me quit the Circle H with her? She knew Keller had orders to kill me . . . Knew I was Jack Halliday . . . I begin to see . . ."

"Having given Keller orders to kill you," Mournful went on, unmindful of the interruption. "Jackson, who never suspects Keller is going around and around with you, schemes this prairie fire. They hadn't had any luck stampeding their stuff into our herd and letting Keller work it; so they gather every Circle H they can find and hold them above us, figuring to start the fire and stampede us back into them. That way they would have had a yell coming and could have demanded that the herds be worked. Keller would have done the job. Don't you see? You can't tell a Circle H from a Rocking Chair at a glance. He'd of got just as many of one as he would of the other. And they were both toting Ringbones."

"There isn't a living soul to thank for blocking their scheme but you, Happy. You bust into that herd of theirs from nowhere and stampede it to hell and gone. That was the only thing on earth Ed Jackson didn't want to happen right then!"

"It was that bronc of Keller's," Happy said. "Good little horse even if it was the out-pitchingest brute ever I forked. It made a run that not many ponies could. I stole him from those lousy rustlers!"

"Sure they're rustlers," Mournful said. "The worst kind. Smart ones. And we've got to thank you for uncovering the whole deal. We've got most of the stuff they rustled last year from Jackson right here in our herd and proof a-plenty it belongs to the Rocking Chair. Jackson and Keller are both dead. We're much obliged to you."

"We?" flashed Happy suspiciously. "Who do you mean, we?"

"Why, her and me, of course," Mournful answered in surprise.

"Are you—already—married?" Happy demanded blankly.

Mournful gulped, looked at the girl. "Lord, no, kid," he said. "You recklect the first day you mentioned the fact that the Old Man had hired a detective to try and get the lowdown on that herd Jackson lost—an old Texas ranger?"

"Yes, but—"

"Meet the gent, kid!" Mournful exclaimed, extending his hand. "I'm not really the *segundo* of this outfit. I'm Jim LeRoy, traveling under the name of Clee Davis—Mournful to you. I'm that range detective you'd never seen."

"You a range detective?" gasped Happy. "You, a hunch-playing old codger with occult power; a—"

"Never had a hunch in my whole life!" Mournful snorted. "Nor occult power, either. I sprung that stuff just to try and tip you off. I sized you up as a square-shooter from the jump. I'd of come plumb clean with you but the Old Man wouldn't let me. So I went to hunch-playing, trying to wise you up that way. You gave me the horse-laugh. But you notice all of those hunches came true. When she," indicating Goldie, "sprung that stuff about a dark man she wasn't talking through her hat. She was trying to tip you off too. We knew before we left Halfway what was up." A twinkle which seemed sadly out of place crept into his faded eyes.

"I looked at you hard many a time trying to figure out if you're serious or joking. I never knew. Sometimes I thought you were wise to my game. The name you found on those case goods at the Circle H was the link we needed to ferret this thing out. We couldn't figure who was paying off at that spread.

"But we did know just how the rustling deal last spring was pulled—how Keller yanked the wool over the eyes of the Rocking Chair punchers. So we was all set for that. And Keller, the stock inspector, was the dark jasper. I kept harping on him continually trying to wise you up. I knew he had orders to bump Jack Halliday off. She," he nodded toward the girl, "found a lot of it out from Jackson himself, who, when he was delirious, spilled his innards too—bragged about how he'd recognized you the minute he laid eyes on you. How he'd fixed it to send Jack Halliday across the divide if he ever got him into the badlands. You know why, of course, kid."

"No!"

" 'Cause Ed Jackson killed your father. He squealed on himself in his delirium. Well," he broke off wearily, "here comes the boys. Reckon the fire's out. You'll have to handle the herd without me, kid—till I get these Circle H jaspers to town and turn Jackson's and Keller's bodies over to the coroner."

"You'll be back?" Happy asked.

"I'm going to stick with you till you take that herd and the Circle H's clean through to summer range and back to the Rocking Chair."

"Mournful," Happy said with feeling. "I'm not joshing myself, I think Goldie's about the finest girl ever I know." He cast an uneasy, sidelong glance at the girl, who met his eyes frankly, "And I'd be plumb proud to call her—aw hell, I'd be proud if she'd even look at me. But she can't see anybody but you. You've won her fair and square. Any girl who will swim the Powder River for a fellow is the gamest little sport on earth."

Mournful burst into laughter. "If all that stammering means you're trying to tell me you're stuck on her, but figure she belongs to me, I'm much obliged. But I don't want her. She swam the Powder to warn me the big boss, whoever he was, was coming to the Circle H and they were planning to knock off our whole herd—wormed it out of Keller some way when he was drunk. You see, she isn't Goldie Burton. No matter what name she had to go under she's just Helen LeRoy. She's my sister and always works with me."

"Your sister!" demanded Happy incredulously. "No wonder she wanted to get away from the Circle H and take me with her. But what the devil did you try to make me believe you were in love with her for?"

"I never said I was in love with her!" Mournful interrupted. "It was you jumped at that conclusion. I told you she wasn't worrying me any. The Old Man was paying for it. We were pulling together in Halfway."

"And—she's—just—your—sister!" Happy repeated in a hollow tone.

"Sure, she's my sister. She's been boarding up here on the south rim of the river since she left Halfway, getting a line on things, before the Old Man sent the herd in. That's how come I knew everything. Fact is, it's just like you said. I didn't know I had occult power until she told me. She's the occult power."

But Happy had ceased to listen. Wheeling he walked away a short distance. Springing up, the girl followed. Slipping her arm into his she said shyly, "I'm sorry I called you a coward back at the Circle H."

"Goldie," he gulped. "Could you—could—"

"Could I?" she exclaimed happily. "Just ask me and see."

"There's a three-way split on that twenty-five hundred dollar reward the Old Man offered for this lost herd for you kids to start out on," Mournful shouted after them. "I'm claiming the thousand dollars for Ed Jackson, the man who killed Jack Halliday."

But the two scarcely heard him. The girl's arms had slipped up around Happy's neck. With his good arm he drew her close and kissed her.

Center Point Large Print
600 Brooks Road / PO Box 1
Thorndike, ME 04986-0001 USA

(207) 568-3717

US & Canada:
1 800 929-9108
www.centerpointlargeprint.com